"Susan K. Salzer writes with a fresh and authentic voice about the brutal turmoil in Missouri during the Civil War. Amid bushwhackers, freebooters, Jayhawkers, guerillas, ruffians, and rascals, young Hattie Rood's care for the wounded teenager, Jesse James, forms an imperiled eye in the storm of war."

Lucia St. Clair Robson, *Ghost Warrior* and *Ride the Wind*

"Like Daniel Woodrell's *Woe to Live On* and Michael Zimmer's *Dust and Glory*, Susan K. Salzer's *Up From Thunder* captures the essence, heartbreak, and humor of western Missouri during the Civil War. *Up From Thunder* is a tremendous debut, and Hattie Rood is an engaging heroine."

Johnny D. Boggs, *Northfield* and *Camp Ford*

"In Hattie Rood, Susan K. Salzer has created a vibrant character—a young woman who learns the true meanings of courage, honor, and love, in the world around her and in herself, all set against the horrific backdrop of Missouri's guerilla wars. Hattie is a great character, and *Up From Thunder* is a wonderful novel."

Thomas Cobb, *Crazy Heart* and *Shavetail*

UP FROM THUNDER

SUSAN K. SALZER

A Cave Hollow Press Book

Warrensburg, Missouri   2010

Up From Thunder

ISBN 0-9713497-5-4
ISBN 978-0-9713497-5-9
Library of Congress Control Number: 2009931113

Copyright © 2010 by Susan K. Salzer

Cover art by Georgia R. Nagel

Except for short passages used in critical articles or reviews, no part of this book may be reproduced or transmitted in any form or by any means, electronic or mechanical, including photo-copying, recording, or by any information storage and retrieval system, without permission in writing from the publisher. For information, write:
Cave Hollow Press
304 Grover Street
Warrensburg, MO 64093.

Cave Hollow Press
Warrensburg, MO

10 9 8 7 6 5 4 3 2 1

For Bill

UP FROM THUNDER

Chapter One

Fever was on the country that long summer, and I do not mean Mr. Lincoln's war but the medical kind. I was myself afflicted with a head that pounded like a blacksmith's hammer and muscles knotted tight as rope. This was my condition the night they brought him to the house, a night I remember clear as yesterday. It was August of my sixteenth year and hot as Egypt. I lay sleepless in my bed, my face to the open window, praying for a breeze. A moon white as bleached bone filled my room with silvery light.

I heard them coming from a long way off, all the way from where our road left the river pike. At first I thought it was just the fever ringing in my head, but then I knew the unmistakable rattle and bang of a wagon's iron tires and the rhythmic clop-clop of horses' feet on the hard dirt. Southern men—they had to be. Federal militia were brave enough when the sun was shining, but nights in our part of Missouri belonged to the bushwhackers—to wild and shadowy men with names like Quantrill, Anderson, Todd, Thrailkill and Thornton—and woe to any soul who denied their sovereignty.

I pulled myself to the window and saw Pa outside near the yard rails holding a pierced tin lantern that swung in his hand, throwing crazy patterns on the ground.

"Who is it, Pa?"

He stood with his back to me, facing the gray ribbon of

road that trailed away into the dark of the woods.

"Anderson's boys," he said. "I got word earlier we might expect company."

This was unwelcome news. Bill Anderson was a devil, and this was true no matter which side of the fight you were on. Just last month he and his men caught old Hiram Griffith out behind his plow and slit his throat from ear to ear leaving him to die in the dirt like a pig. This because Anderson suspected him of aiding the Yanks, which he probably was not, as Hiram was a Southern man. And eighteen-year-old Soloman Baum, whose wife just had a baby, they hung from a beam in his barn for the same reason. I thought of Hiram and Sol as our visitors formed up from the gloom like mounted apparitions; two horsemen followed by a mule-drawn wagon.

Pa walked forward to meet them.

"Well all right," he said in a low voice. "Bring him in. He can stay here till he dies or gets better."

The horsemen dismounted and lifted a body from the back of the wagon. As they passed under my window the light of Pa's lantern fell on the wounded man's face. I say man, but he was a boy really, of about my age it would seem, and bad hurt by the look of him.

"Hang on, Dingus," the taller of his two bearers said as they entered the house. I was struck by the tender notes in his voice. "Zerel will skin me alive if anything happens to you."

A trail of black blood on the porch steps marked their passage.

I returned to my bed and stared at the cold, watchful moon. If the Federals found those boys here they'd hang Pa from the nearest tree and fire our place. Already they'd tried to burn us out the year before, right after that trouble in Lawrence, and they almost succeeded too. Would have, if not for a provident rainfall.

"There's a loft upstairs above my daughter's room," I heard Pa say. "Your brother will be safe up there."

One of the men laughed.

"Safe and cooked too! That loft will be like a oven in this heat!" he said. "Dead is dead, one way or another. Let's take him with us, Frank."

"Shut up, Jim." This second voice was deeper, more commanding. "The accommodation you offer will do just fine. Thank you for your generosity, Captain Rood, and I hope not to inconvenience you for long. Our uncle's gone to fetch a doctor from Kansas City, a friend to the family. Meantime I'll send some boys over to help you folks with the nursing."

I wanted to yell down to Pa to send those fellows packing, and the hurt one too, but I knew it wouldn't do no good. Pa was thinking about what he would want done if it was my brother, Doak, lying in some stranger's farmhouse seeking succor. Deep-down I guess I felt the same, but it didn't make me any less afraid.

I climbed out of bed and shuffled over to Doak's empty room cross the hall. The only way to the loft was through a trap door in my closet, and I couldn't countenance letting strange men see me in only a summer chemise.

I settled in Doak's bed, pulling the counterpane up to my chin despite the heat. He'd been gone more than a year now but his bed still bore the smell of him, a mix of tobacco that he smoked on the sly and sun-dried clothes. That smell knifed me—we hadn't heard from him since before Christmas, and there were so many ways for a boy to die nowadays.

It took some flipping around to get comfortable. Doak's bed wasn't good as mine; the support ropes were slack, and the tick needed fresh hay but, then those things seemed not to matter to him. Doak, he could sleep like a ghost any where, any time. Me, I was different that way.

The two men had a struggle carrying the other up the short ladder to the loft. Then there was swearing and grunting and banging around, and then many trips up and down to the kitchen to get him set up. The eastern sky was pinking up when at last they took their leave. It wasn't until then that I finally slept, only to dream of Pharaoh's army chasing the Israelites through a parted sea—though in my dream the water didn't close back on Pharaoh's soldiers like it was supposed to.

The sun was fully up when Pa woke me. He looked like he'd been awake all night, which I guess he had, with purple hollows below his eyes attesting to his weariness.

"How are you this morning, Hattie?" He set a bowl of oatmeal on the table by the bed.

"Better, Pa. Much better."

This was untrue; if anything I felt worse than yesterday, but what good would it do to say so?

"What about him?" I pointed to the loft above. "He going to live?"

Pa shrugged.

"Coin's still in the air. He took it here." He put his hand on the right side of his own bony chest. "The bullet went clean through, and that's to the good, but he bled a good amount. Can you tend him today while me and Cy work the field?"

"Surely, Pa."

Poor Pa. I wanted to help him all I could on account of he'd had more than his ration of sorrow. The past five years had aged him twenty. Ma died just before the war started, withering to bone from an ailment no doctor could name. In '61 my oldest brother, Ben, was killed by a Yankee sharpshooter at Wilson's Creek and now Doak was gone for a soldier too. Pa was brave but he was fighting a losing battle with heartbreak, constant toil, and worry.

Me, I worried too, but mostly I was angry. I wanted things to be the way they used to be before all this trouble came to us. I wanted it to be how it was before the war when Pa farmed hemp and made good money selling to sailcloth manufacturers and to the St. Louis ropewalks who made baling twine for the cotton growers down South. But the aggression of Abe Lincoln and his Black Republicans put an end to all that, so Pa switched our fields over to tobacco. This was backbreaking work, blood, sweat, and tears work, and Pa had only old, one-eyed Cyrus to help him, now Doak was gone. Cy wasn't much by way of help, but with the shortage of able-bodied men in Missouri nowadays, we were lucky to have even him.

So yes, I wanted to help Pa all I could.

"I can milk Eugenie too," I said.

"You're a brave girl, Hattie." He covered my hand with his rough, dry paw. "Your mother would be proud."

"Yes, Pa." The Ma I remembered never seemed to take much pride in anything about me except for my red-colored hair, which I got from her anyhow. "It's your glory, Hattie," she used to say to me as she brushed it, which she did every night. "Your beautiful hair will prove your glory." I never liked it when she said that, because I figured to have more glory to me than just a head of red hair.

For a girl I had a lot of steel in my nature. I prized this in myself above all other traits. I could work longer and harder than other girls, I could run, ride, and swim good as any boy—better than some—and I wasn't afraid of snakes or bugs. If she valued any of these qualities in me, she never said.

After Pa left I forced down a cold clump of oatmeal, then reached for the blue gingham dress I wore yesterday and the day before that. It hung on me like rags on a scarecrow. If not for my color I'd look like one of old man Craighead's skinny nigra slave girls working his tobacco in their faded hand-me-down dresses. This, my raggedy wardrobe, I felt to be a grave injustice. Somewhere girls my age were dressing for the day in petticoats and crinolines and Garibaldi dresses with dropped shoulders and leg o' mutton sleeves. Oh, I knew about those things. I saw them in *Godey's Lady's Book*, drawings of elegant ladies in gowns cut low to show off their shoulders and bosom and high collarbones. I didn't have much bosom, but I had good shoulders and collarbones. I'd turn a man's head in a dress like that, I knew I would, and someday I'd have one. Someday, when this war was over and these wild murderous men who had taken Missouri—Federals and Secesh—were dead or gone back to wherever they came from...

As I finished dressing I remembered the boy upstairs and

wondered if he was still alive. Well, if he was he'd have to wait. Eugenie, our lone remaining milk cow, stood in the barnyard, her bag full to bursting. I'd have to tend her before checking our visitor.

Hot as it was the night before, the morning had cooled off some. A rain was heading our way. I thought of Doak as I walked to the barn, remembering a cool fall morning like this years before when we rode our sweet sorrel palfrey over to Uncle Hi Braddock's place to steal apples. Hi Braddock was nobody's uncle far as I knew but everyone called him that, even the grown-ups. We brought the apples back for Ma who made a pie—a fine cinnamon pie with raisins and a short, buttery crust that melted in your mouth—and we ate it warm from the oven with that morning's cream poured over each slice. Just thinking of that pie now, with nothing but Pa's oatmeal in my stomach, made me feel very sorry for myself.

Eugenie met me at the gate, anxious to be relieved of her burden. She followed me to the sturdy log barn Pa built with his two sons back when things were good. It was the best barn in Ray County, bar none, strong and warm in the winter because of the way Pa had the boys bank the earth up around the bottom to shore up the foundation and block out that mean iron wind that blows down off the plains of Nebraska Territory every year come January.

I took the stool from its peg on the wall and set it down in its regular place. Eugenie came swinging to me ready to get started. My head was swimmy from illness and I leaned my cheek against her hairy side as I worked, comforted by her earthy smell. Her swollen bag was hot to the touch; the milk jetted from her teats, hitting the bottom of the pail like a tin drum. My thoughts drifted back to the boy in the loft. What sort was he? Good-looking from what little I saw, but what sort? Was he kind and funny, or the type who deserved to suffer? Was he suffering, dying maybe, even now as I milked the cow?

Before leaving the barnyard I stopped to pour a little milk

into an old skillet we kept by the gate for the dog, Earl Smith. We called him that because his doggy features and long knobby limbs resembled those of a neighbor farmer by that name. Me and Doak, we found Earl Smith—the dog that is—wandering through the scrub by the river, a dog skeleton mostly, with a piece of rawhide tied down fast over his eyes. Some bad boy's idea of a joke, I reckon. Anyhow, we brought Earl home, fed him up, and now he was a sassy pup with an inflated notion of his own importance. Earl was a smiler though not wanton with his doggy favors. Other than me and Doak, very few were greeted with a curl of Earl's whiskery lip. Not even Pa.

In the kitchen I set the milk pail on the table, covered it with cheesecloth to keep out the flies and prepared myself for the climb to the loft. I was fearful of what I might find up there, not because I had any great love for bushwhackers—they were mostly Freebooters in fancy embroidered shirts—but because I did not relish the prospect of finding a handsome Missouri boy reduced to a bled-out corpse.

The short ladder to the loft was still in place, the trap door open. I took a deep breath, climbed the four steps, and stuck my head through the opening.

The tiny room had only one window, round, like a ship's porthole, which admitted but a dim light. The boy lay on the far side of the room on a low army cot, a relic of Pa's Mexican War service. At least he was alive; his bare bandaged chest rose and fell with each breath.

I pulled myself through the opening and crawled to the cot. The loft's ceiling was steep and sloping, and not tall enough for standing except at the center. The puncheon floor creaked under my weight as I moved toward him but the boy did not stir. When I got closer I saw that he was indeed handsome, with light brown hair worn long in the Southern way and cheekbones high as a red Indian's. On the floor beside him lay a pistol belt with two holstered .36 caliber Colt Navies—I knew my guns—and a bloody border shirt. The bushwhacker boys all wore such shirts, with deep breast pockets for powder charges, lead balls, and spare, preloaded cylinders. The handwork on this shirt was especially fine—green garlands with red and blue flowers carefully stitched across the front and around the cuffs. A mother's work? A sweetheart's? He surely wasn't old enough for a wife.

I was leaning over him almost nose-to-nose when he opened his eyes and looked straight at me. His eyes were shockingly blue, blue as the cornflowers my Ma used to grow in her summer garden. I jumped back, banging my head on a rafter beam hard enough to start tears in my eyes.

"Where am I?" he said. His voice was croaky, a whisper.

"Ray County. In the home of Captain John Rood, my father."

He closed his eyes. "I am dry as a chip."

There was a tin mug and a pitcher of water on the floor by the window. I filled the mug and held it out to him, but he was too weak to take it, too weak even to raise his head, so I put my hand under his head and lifted. His hair was soft and damp with sweat. He drained the cup in two gulps and ran his tongue over cracked lips.

"What happened?" I said. "Did the Yankees do this to you?"

He shook his head.

"Some Dutchman," he said. "I needed a saddle."

I put two and two together and figured the shooter must have been Fritz Heizinger, a German immigrant who farmed the bottoms five miles up the road. He was the only Dutchman left in these parts, his brethren having pulled up stakes and moved to Kansas where the citizenry was friendlier to his kind. Like all Germans Fritz was a Unionist, but I liked him anyhow. He gave us cheese and eggs when he had them to spare. I surely wished him no harm.

"What did you do?" I said. "Did you boys kill him?"

The boy moved his head again, barely, as if the motion pained him.

"He took off, hid in a cornfield."

They must have been stealing from him; Fritz wouldn't shoot otherwise. This insight filled me with righteous steam.

"You bushwhackers oughtn't go taking from folks who got it hard enough already," I said. "You should be fighting with the regulars like my brother. You should be down in Arkansas with General Sterling Price."

He turned those blue eyes on me. "Regulars have too many rules," he said.

"You boys could use some rules, way I see it."

By now my exertions were getting the best of me. I set the pitcher by the cot and crawled toward the loft door. I felt creaky and stiff as an old granny.

"I'm in the room below you," I said. "Pound on the floor with this if you need anything."

I took granddaddy's walking stick from the corner and slid it to him.

"Wait," he said as I started down the ladder. "How do I call you? What's your name?"

"I am Henrietta Rood but you may call me Hattie."

"I'm Jesse. Jesse W. James, of Clay County. Pleased to make your acquaintance, Hattie."

Chapter Two

A feeble thumping woke me mid-afternoon from a thick sleep. My head was stuffed with cotton, and some time passed before I recognized what the sound was and who was making it. My room was hot and airless with bright sunlight streaming through the dormer window. I didn't want to get up, but I knew I had to. Bad as it was in here, it had to be twenty times hotter in that loft.

Somehow I managed to hoist myself up the ladder. It was perilous going; my bones felt thin and snappable beneath my skin.

A groan of relief greeted me as I stuck my head through the trap door. The loft was dark and rank. The animal smell reminded me of the big cat cage at the zoo Pa took me and the boys to in St. Louis that time.

"I thought you'd never come," he said. "I need water."

I went to his bedside and looked in the pitcher. It wasn't empty.

"I'm sorry," he said, and even in the low light I could see him go red. "There wasn't nothing else to use."

Pa or one of them bushwhackers who brought him up here should've thought of that, but I'd already learned men were not insightful when it came to such matters.

"Never mind it," I said. "We're all God's creatures. Anyhow, I grew up with two brothers. I'm no shrinking violet."

The trip down the stairs and out to the well to wash and refill the pitcher took a long time. I was still shaky and wore out. I sat on the chair by the kitchen door and took a long drink myself before heading back. Earl Smith joined me, looking up with sorrowing brown eyes that said, "These are hard times."

I scratched his scarred, floppy ears. I was his favorite person. I knew this not only because I got the most smiles, but because he was forever taking my things back to his nest under the porch. When something went missing I knew I'd find it there: my hairbrush, my shawl, a pair of drawers. Pa said I ought to beat Earl for this but how could I beat a creature who valued me so highly he loved even the smell of me?

"I won't do it, Earl," I said out loud. "I won't never beat you."

Back in the loft Jesse drank two full cups of water and would've taken more if I'd let him.

"Best let that soak in first," I said. "If you drink too much, it'll just come back up."

He nodded and wiped his mouth with the back of his hand. I noticed then that the tip of his left middle finger was missing, not a recent injury but an old, well-healed one. Beyond this, there was not much wrong with him, physique-wise anyhow. He was a muscular and broad-shouldered boy, by appearance strong and not the sort to run from a fight. How much fight was left in him, I wondered?

At the moment he was looking pretty peaked. His skin was ghost-pale and clammy and the dark under his eyes looked like bruises. The muslin bandage around his chest was soaked with blood and needed changing. I had some experience with this sort of thing, having tended Pa the previous summer when he was shot by a band of raggedy-ass Missouri Enrolled Militia who'd come looking for my brother. Doak was already gone with Price's army and the Yanks were denied that satisfaction, so they put a bullet in Pa and torched our barn for their trouble. Like I said, if not for the rain that came just after they left our whole enterprise would've gone up, barn, house, outbuildings, the whole outfit. Somehow I got Pa in the buckboard and drove him over to Heizinger's place. It was Fritz who showed me how to clean a wound properly, how to dry wet, suppurating flesh with sugar, how to pack a bullet hole with lint to keep it open and draining. So, yes, I could doctor Jesse's wound all right.

Pa's medicine bag was in the corner. Inside I found everything I needed; scissors, bandages, plasters, lint I'd made myself from the scrapings of old linen underwear, folded paper packets of sugar.

"Last night your brother said one of your relatives was going to Kansas City to fetch a doctor." I decided to keep talking to distract him as my ministrations were like to be painful. "Your uncle, he said it was."

A blue light of hope kindled in his eyes.

"Buck said that? Thomas James is bringing a doctor?"

"If Buck is your brother, then yes he said it. Don't you remember?"

"I don't remember nothing—nothing but pain—after him and Jim Cummins put me in that wagon. I half hoped the Yanks would catch us just to end my misery."

He went even paler at the memory.

"Well, that's all over now," I said. Gently as I could I pulled the muslin away from the wound. I had to tug some, as it wanted to stick, but finally I got it free. Just the sight of that wound made my insides pucker. He'd taken a large-caliber bullet right below the right nipple. Pa said the bullet went clean through; now it was a finger-size black hole with proud red flesh all around.

"You're a lucky one, you are," I said.

He smiled a half-smile. "I don't feel too lucky just now."

"Well, the bullet went clean through, that's one way you're lucky. Another, your lung wasn't popped. If it was, there'd be bloody foam coming up out of that hole." I said this, though the bullet must indeed have penetrated his lung; given its location, it had to. Still, the lack of froth I took to be a good sign. I had seen this when my cousin Schuyler was accidentally shot by his own brother one fall afternoon when the three of us were out rabbit hunting. Watching a fun-loving ten-year-old boy leave this world terrified and suffocating in his own juices was a thing I hope never to see the like of again.

"And you got me looking out for you," I added. "That's a third."

"And the most important, I reckon," he said, again with the smile.

After the front hole was clean I helped Jess roll over and tended the exit wound on his back. This was a messier business but not too bad. Being a red-blooded Missouri girl I couldn't help but notice his shoulders were broad and strong-looking and browned by the sun. Strong shoulders are a good sign in a man, an indicator he's not afraid of hard work.

"You've a gentle touch, Miss Hattie," he said as I wrapped a clean length of muslin around him. I liked the way he spoke my name.

"Just Hattie," I said. "You can drop the 'miss' part."

I held his head as he took another mug of water. My hand must have shook some for he sensed something was wrong. He asked me about it.

"I been sick," I said. "Breakbone fever the doctor called it and it is rightly named. I will testify to that."

I expected his next question to be, "is it catching?" but he didn't say anything. Instead he just laid his head back on the blue tick pillow and closed his eyes. The pillow, like the mattress underneath it, was stuffed with straw and not much of it. He didn't care; within minutes he was sound asleep. I went back to my bed and stared at the ceiling, thinking about Jesse and his brother, Frank. I still wasn't sure what sort they were.

You see, Clay County boys were hard cases, rougher than most. That was because folks along the Kansas line had been fighting the slavery question for a long time, long as I can remember, years before Ape Lincoln started his war over it. Me, I don't love slavery, I know it's not right to own another human like you would a wagon or a farm animal, but it's also not right the way Jayhawkers and abolitionist Negro thieves raid over into Missouri to take what's ours.

I understood why menfolk in Clay and those other border counties formed up in social clubs like the Blue Lodges and Sons of the South and started militating, setting up combat training camps in the bush of Clay County and the Sni Hills of Jackson. Even so, some went too far, threatening to "Mormonize" the Abolitionists and everybody knew what that meant. It wasn't so long ago when the people of northwest Missouri rose up to drive the Mormons—Danites, to my granddaddy—out of our state. Danites, Mormons, whatever you call them, those people were clannish and money-loving and had some mighty strange ideas about angels and golden tablets and whatnot, but even so an army of worked-up Missouri men did things to them, also to their women and children, that brought us no glory. Were Jesse and his brother of that radical stripe?

I must've fallen asleep wondering because the sound of horses woke me at sundown. From my bedroom window I saw two men below in the yard. They rode fine strong horses, a sure sign they were bushwhackers since no one else in these parts had horses like that these days.

One of the men, the bigger of the two, saw me and lifted his sweat-stained black hat.

"Evening, miss," he said, inclining his head like a gentleman passing on the street. "I'm Ol Shepherd and this here is Nat Tigue. We're here to help you all care for the boy. Jesse."

Two more mouths to feed was the last thing we needed and these fellows didn't look like much by way of nursemaids anyhow.

"Thank you all the same," I said, "but me and Pa can take care of him on our own."

The big man, Ol, smiled.

"No," he said, dismounting and gesturing for his companion to do the same. "I guess we'll be stayin'. The boss told us to nurse our boy Dingus and that's what we'll do."

"Your boss?"

"William T. Anderson, miss. Bill Anderson has the say-so nowadays. Ain't that so, Nat?"

Nat spit on the ground and grinned up at me, his eyes narrow as slits in a mask.

"That is so," he said. "Bloody Bill makes the rules nowadays."

Chapter Three

Border ruffians, bushwhackers, guerillas, partisan rangers—people called them by different names, but they were cast from the same mold: they were all Missouri boys for the South, fighting under a black flag.

William Quantrill was the most famous of the lot but despite his fame he was a cypher. Nobody knew his story, not for sure. Some said he was a schoolteacher from Maryland who hated Jayhawkers on account of they murdered his older brother before the war. Others say he's nothing more than a Kansas cattle rustler and slave thief who snuck across the border at night to steal slaves from Missourians and then sold them back to their owners for a handsome profit. One thing everyone agreed on: Quantrill was a crack shot and superb horseman with balls like a brass monkey. (Not a ladylike description, but that's how they said it.) He was the idea man behind that business last summer when hundreds of Missouri guerillas rode into Lawrence at dawn to murder some one hundred fifty men and boys. That raid made Quantrill king of the bushwhackers and terror of abolitionist freestaters, but it was his undoing, too, because many people, including decent Southerners like me and Pa and Doak, were disgusted by the unfairness of it, the randomness of the killing. Even some of the boys who rode with him were troubled by it, or so I've heard it said.

I had a personal encounter with Quantrill, without knowing it, one morning not too long before Jesse came to us. I was outdoors hanging wash when two riders, a man and a woman, helloed the house. The man was tall and lanky with long, light-colored hair, the woman wore a cloak. I walked out to meet them with one hand on the loaded pistol I carried always in my waist pocket. Earl Smith came with me, bristling along his bony spine.

The man lifted his hat and favored me with a smile. He was fine-looking, to be sure, clean-shaven with an easy charm, though maybe a touch girlish in the face. His eyes were of the palest blue and hooded like a red man's.

"Good morning, miss," he said. "My wife and I wonder if we might refresh ourselves at your well. Traveling in this heat is dry work. If you'll permit, I'd like to water the horses as well."

I was suspicious. The horses were top notch and the woman jumpy as a cat. She tried to hide it, acting friendly like her man, but her eyes kept cutting back to the road like someone was after them. It would not serve to rile them, no matter who they were.

"Help yourself," I said. "Our well has the sweetest water in Ray County, and you are welcome to it." I pointed to the barnyard where Eugenie watched us with mild curiosity. "Your horses can drink from the trough."

"You are very kind," the man said, dismounting gracefully like one who spent much time in the saddle. He led the horses to their drink, then joined the woman at the well. When they had their fill the woman asked to use our privy.

"Nice place," he said. His eyes were taking it all in and I could see they were not the kind that missed much. "Lot of work though. You must have a large family?"

I wasn't born yesterday. He wanted to know if there were any men around and if so, how many.

"Oh I do. My father and three brothers." Actually, it was down to just me and Pa by then but I wasn't going to proclaim such to this smooth stranger.

"Brothers? They haven't joined the fight then?"

Now he was fishing for which side we favored but I wasn't going to fall for this either. A person could get shot, just for answering wrong.

"Not for just now," said I.

Earl was sniffing round the stranger's feet and he bent down to scratch his ears. I noticed Earl allowed it, and even took some comfort in it as he was generally a solid judge of character. All the while, though, the man's Indian eyes were studying our house, the barn, the field where Pa and Cy were working, out of sight. The buildings wanted paint and the fence rails sagged. When he turned his eyes back on me there was a smile in them, like I hadn't fooled him any.

I said, "So where are you and your wife headed?" I was relieved that my voice did not reveal my nervousness.

He hesitated.

"East," he said. "To Howard County. Kate and I will set up housekeeping in the Perche Hills. I hear it's cooler there."

I nodded, understanding he did not refer to the weather.

His wife returned and they prepared to resume their journey. Before remounting his horse, he took my hand and pressed a coin into my palm. Opening my fingers I saw a shiny gold double eagle worth twenty-five dollars!

"You don't have to, mister," I said.

"Perhaps not but I want to thank you for your hospitality." He smiled down at me from the saddle. "You took a chance on us and I am grateful for it, but from now on I advise you to be more cautious. The country is full of dangerous men. Bushwhackers and the like."

He may have winked at me as he said this; I wasn't sure.

"Yes sir, I will. And thank you, Mr..."

"Hart. Charley Hart."

The name meant nothing to me then. Only later did I learn that Charley Hart was what Quantrill called himself when his real name would not suit. I also learned that his woman, Kate, was nervous because George Todd, Bill Anderson, and others of Quantrill's lieutenants had mutinied against him and relations were no longer cordial. From that point on, Anderson and Todd led their own bands and by all accounts these fellows were more ruthless than their former leader.

So Quantrill was the most famous bushwhacker, but by the time Jesse came to us Anderson was the most feared. They said he was handsome as a stage actor with dark, curling hair that fell to his shoulders, a thin mustache, and a beard he was vain about, keeping it nicely trimmed even in the bush. He dressed entirely in black, sometimes black velvet, and he rode a black horse. People who should know said he frothed at the mouth when he rode into battle and kept count of his killings with knots on a silken cord he wore round his waist.

Unlike other bushwhackers, Anderson penned long letters to the Lexington newspapers, rants more like it, filled with boasts, taunts, and threats, the ramblings of a madman. I sent one of those newspaper letters to Doak asking him to show it to Sterling Price in hopes he would pass it along to Jeff Davis and them. Maybe if the Confederate leaders in Richmond knew what us folks in Missouri were up against, then maybe they would do something about it.

> *Mr. Editors: In reading both your papers I see you urge the policy of the citizens taking up arms to defend their persons and property. You are only asking them to sign their death warrants...Listen to me, fellow citizens; do not obey this last order. Do not take up arms if you value your lives and property. It is not in my power to save your lives if you do. If you proclaim to be in arms against the guerillas I will kill you. I will hunt you down like wolves and murder you. You cannot escape...Be careful how you act for my eyes are upon you...*

It was true what the newspapers said. "The devil is loose

in these parts with scarcely three feet of chain to his neck." We were in a dangerous place, me and Pa, saddled with three of Bloody Bill's boys with Federal patrols and militia all around. From the get-go it was clear to me that Nat and Ol weren't interested in caring for their sick friend. Oh, they looked in on him from time to time, to make sure he had not given up the ghost, but that's far as it went. I didn't know for sure why Bloody Bill sent them but I thought it could be to keep an eye on me and Pa while Jesse recovered. Could be Anderson doubted our loyalty, worried we might rat them out to the Federals. We would never, but it was true I was heartily, fervently sick of bushwhackers and Yankees alike.

Yes, I was in a peevish state of mind. This may have been due to my illness and generally run-down condition, or it may have resulted from the discontent that plagued me while lying in my sickbed. I had too much time then to dream and aspire and my aspirations were so far removed from my current situation, well, it made me sour. In my imagining I was traveling with a wagon caravan going north and west to the new Montana Territory Cy had told me so much about. He had been out there, old one-eyed Cy, and he spoke of mountains so high they had snowy tops even in summer, of streams flowing down from those mountains clean as crystal, full of trout, and so cold you couldn't hardly hold that fish in your hands once you caught it. Even the sky is different from what we got here in Missouri, Cy said, bigger and bluer, and on clear days you can see clean to the place where the earth bends away. At night the sky glows with colors, a heavenly rainbow called the avoli boralits or some such, and oh! how I longed to see this! The valleys are thick with native grains so lush and tall they brush your horse's belly when you ride through, and wild strawberries grow along the river banks.

So I dreamed of Montana when I lay abed, sweating with fever. And the truth of it was I dreamed of going alone—well, with Earl Smith and maybe Doak—but for sure without Pa or Joe Craighead, the boy I was supposed to marry. Not that I didn't care for them, of course I did, I just didn't need them to be part of my new life, not right away anyhow. And because of my steel, I would not be afraid either, not a bit, even though there were red Indians out there who would do terrible things to a white woman if they caught her. No, red Indians would not stop me. Way I saw it, no red man could be worse than the white ones we had here in Missouri.

The day after Nat and Ol showed up, Frank, Jesse's brother, returned. It was sundown and I'd just taken a plate of supper up to the loft when I heard him ride up. Nat, who did nothing all day but sit on the porch carving on a piece of wood and watching the road, ran out to meet him. They had a short, vigorous talk about something, then Frank climbed up to the loft. The sloping ceiling was too low to accommodate his height, so he came stooping, hat in hand, to the bedside.

"How is he?" he said. His weathered face creased with worry as he looked down on his sleeping brother.

"Not good," I said. Jesse's condition had worsened since I checked him a few hours before. His breathing was fast and shallow and he didn't seem to know we were there. "When's that doctor coming?"

"Soon. It doesn't take that long to get here from Kansas City—leastways not if a man's in the proper hurry."

I hoped he was, for Jesse's sake and the doctor's, too. Things would go hard on him if Jesse went south because a sawbones dawdled.

Frank touched his brother's cheek with the back of his hand, a mother's gesture.

"He's burning up. Is he infected?"

"He could be. The flesh is proud and I saw no granulations."

Granules, like little sugar crystals around a wound, were a sign of healing.

Frank's gray eyes met mine. He had a long mournful face, and his winged-out ears made his head look like a two-handled teacup. Brother Jesse got the good looks in the James family, that was sure.

"Maybe I'll hang around for a while," Frank said. "Wait for the doctor to show up. Would that be all right?"

I had no problem with it. Frank was different from Nat and Ol, he had education and manners. I invited him down to sit at the kitchen table with us, but he refused, instead taking up the plate I'd brought for Jesse.

"I'll eat this," he said. "Jess won't. Anyhow I want to be here if he comes round. But I thank you for the kind invitation."

I got supper for Pa and Cy, Nat and Ol. It wasn't much—bacon and rice with skillet cornbread—but they went at it like Sunday dinner at the Planter's House. Me, I had no appetite.

After cleaning up I took a bowl of scraps into the kitchen yard and whistled for Earl. Usually he was waiting for me at the door, but not tonight. I whistled again and called his name, yet still he didn't come. I was starting to worry when I heard him making a ruckus in the timber by the river. Nat heard it too, coming out of the house, pistol drawn, with Ol right behind him. Something or someone was crashing through the brush, coming our way. If it was Feds we were in for it. The bushwhackers would fight them to the death with no regard for me and Pa or our property.

But it wasn't Feds. A little man carrying a bag burst out of the woods with Earl Smith nipping at his heels. He ran straight for the house, stopping once to swing a boot at Earl who easily dodged it.

"Doc Ridge? Is that you?"

The voice at my shoulder made me jump. Frank had come on catpaws and now stood behind me, gun in hand. He stepped around me to greet our little visitor.

"Dammit, Frank!" the stranger said. "Of course it's me! Put that gun away!"

He was stout and winded from his exertions.

"I'll have you know I had the devil's own time getting here! Patrols are out in force tonight, I had to walk at least a mile from where I hid my horse by the river and if someone doesn't get this damned fyce off me this instant I will put a bullet in its brain!"

Chapter Four

Frank and I took the doctor upstairs. The loft was hot as Hades; Jesse was mumbling on his cot. Ol followed us, carrying a lantern. Doc Ridge kneeled on the floor at Jesse's side and opened up his bag. Ridge had the tiniest hands I had ever seen on a grown man, soft and dimpled at the knuckles like a baby's. They were not hands that inspired confidence.

"What took you so long, Doc?" Frank said crossly. "You walk all the way from Kansas City?"

Ignoring him, Ridge took from his bag a wooden instrument. He put the smaller, belled end to Jesse's bandaged chest and his ear to the other. He listened with his eyes closed, then moved the bell a few inches and listened again. After, he put his fat baby fingers on Jesse's wrist to count his heartbeats. Having done this myself earlier, I knew Jesse's heart was galloping.

Ridge returned to his bag and pulled out a narrow wooden case. Inside was a skinny glass tube, bulbed on one end, with an ivory scale like the kind you see on a weather gauge attached to the body of the thing. I had never seen anything like this before. He slid the bulbed end under Jesse's armpit.

"A thermometer," he said, sensing my interest. "It measures the body's heat."

Jesse remained in a twilight throughout all this, moaning but not speaking.

"As for your question, Franklin," Ridge said, his eyes on the mercury climbing the gauge, "the answer is no, I did not walk from Kansas City. If I was delayed it was because I took precautions and you should be grateful I did so. Yankee patrols are out in force, thick as the fleas on that mangy hound that tried to deliver me into their hands. Your uncle and I set out together from Richmond, but as Thomas James is a known Southern man, I insisted on coming on alone. If confronted I would have been hard pressed to explain our business together."

He removed the glass tube from under Jesse's arm and held it to the light, frowning at the register.

"One hundred four degrees," he said. "Tell me what happened, Frank. You were with him, I assume?"

"I was. It was four days ago, on the 13th. Earlier that day we tangled with a company of Paw Paws down along the Wakenda." Paw Paws—officially Enrolled Missouri Militia—were Federal conscripts, mostly local fellows enlisted in '62 after the Union government forced all able-bodied men between the ages of eighteen and forty-five to join the militia or be considered disloyal. We called them Paw Paws because they liked to hide out in the woods along the rivers amongst the Paw Paw trees. They were not brave. Unlike the Missouri State Militia, these boys were poorly armed and undis-ciplined and would rather be fighting, if they had to fight at all, with their Southern neighbors instead of against them. Naturally, they made a fat target for the bushwhackers who held them in contempt.

"Afterwards Jesse and Jim Cummins and I were riding apart from the others when Jess saw a saddle sitting on a fence rail. He got down off his horse to take it and that's when he got shot. It was a Dutchman, firing on us from his house. We didn't see him till it was too late and then he ran off. Jim and I thought about going after him, but we didn't. Seemed more important to get help for Jesse. We got him back on his horse and he managed to ride about three miles, and then he couldn't so we got a wagon and brought him here."

Ridge turned to me. The lamplight reflected off the flat glass of his spectacles.

"Who's been caring for this boy? You, girl?"

"Yes sir."

"How long has he been fevering like this?"

"He's been low all day, but not this bad. He took two eggs at breakfast and then at noon tea and dry toast."

"Was he coherent?" Ridge said.

Seeing I did not know the word he re-put the question.

"Was he talking? Did he make any sense?"

We had talked about things we liked to eat, extra-special things, and he told me about his mother's blackberry cobbler—how she made it with butter, milk, and sugar and berries from their farm, and baked it in a cast iron skillet then served it warm with cream poured over the top, and he bet me I'd never had anything so tasty in my life. I told him I could make a Jenny Lind cake that would put his mother's cobbler to shame and he said, *This is Missouri so you'll have to show me,* and I said, *I know it.*

"He made sense," I said. "Coherent sense."

Ridge smiled. "Has he taken anything since? Water even?"

I shook my head. "Not since noon."

Ridge fished some scissors from his bag and started cutting through Jesse's chest bandage. As he cut he told Ol to get out of the loft because he wasn't doing anything but holding a lantern and his big body was making the hot room hotter still. I held the lamp over Jesse. As he uncovered the chest wound I caught a bad smell, like meat starting to turn. It scared me. I didn't want that to happen to Jesse.

Ridge went back to his bag and took out a blue bottle with liquid inside.

"Franklin," he said, "pull the cot out into the room, away from the wall. Position yourself at the head of the bed and hold Jesse down by the shoulders. I will purify the wound now and it will be painful."

As if on cue, Jesse moaned.

Ridge turned to me.

"In the future, Miss Rood—and in this Godforsaken world I have no doubt the future will provide you with ample opportunities—begin treatment of a gunshot wound with cold water soaks. Clean the wound as best you can taking particular care to remove any foreign matter—bits of cloth from a shirt or coat, for example—from the tissues. Then keep the flesh wet and thickly bandaged until all signs of inflammation disappear. Only when this occurs do you begin dry bandaging with salves and poultices. Sugar, as you have used, will suit in a pinch but it is at best only mildly efficacious."

My stomach balled up in a fist. Was I responsible for Jesse's condition? Had I, through my ignorance, consigned this fine, broad-shouldered boy to the grave?

My thoughts must have showed on my face because Ridge's next words were meant to comfort me.

"Now, now, do not rebuke yourself, girl." He liked big words but he had a nice smile to go with them. "You did all right. Jesse has been carefully tended. I can see that."

He turned to Frank and uncorked the blue vial. I read the label, written in an apothecary's flourishing hand: Aqua fortis.

"Get ready, Franklin," Ridge said.

Frank kneeled at the head of the cot and pinned his brother by the shoulders. His jaw muscles squared under his stubbly beard.

Ridge poured the contents of the vial onto Jesse's wound. Seconds passed before the pain reached Jesse in his distant, fevered place; he gasped, then cried out, a hoarse animal sound, as smoke rose from the hole. He arched his back and twisted, wild in his agony, but Frank was on his feet now, using all his weight to keep his brother down. Sickened, I backed away, far as I could, as Jesse's flesh sizzled like meat in a skillet. The smell was one I hope never to know again.

"Turn him, Franklin," Ridge said when at last the burning stopped and Jesse lay still. "I will treat the exit wound now."

Unable to watch, I set the lamp on the floor and descended the short ladder to my room where I took refuge on my bed, wrapping the thick feather pillow about my head and pressing it tight to my ears. But even this was not sufficient to defeat the sound of Jesse's animal cries.

Chapter Five

Nat and Ol requested Doc Ridge's services once he was done with Jesse. Ol had an angry boil on his neck that wanted lancing and Nat had some private, man problem that I supposed was Venus-related though it truly made me sick to think of mean-eyed Nat in the throes of an amorous passion.

Anyhow, it was near midnight when Ridge finally took his leave. Me, Pa, and Frank sat down with him at the kitchen table to receive his medical instructions. Despite the cool night air, Ridge's forehead and upper lip were beaded with sweat.

"Miss Rood, I will leave you two medicines." He set his bag on the table, took out a small green bottle with a cork stopper and gave it to me.

"Laudanum," he said, "for his pain. Administer it sparingly, as needed. It will help him sleep."

Then he gave me a second bottle, clear, with a colorless liquid inside.

"And this is quinine. He is to receive one-half teaspoon every hour. If his fever is caused by infection, as I fear it is, this will have no effect. But if some contagion is the root of it—perhaps the breakbone fever that afflicts the area—it will help."

I accepted this second bottle with a shudder. Quinine had been forced on me during my bout with illness; it was bitter as wormwood and produced a loud ringing in the ears that continued for days. Jesse might take one dose of this, but it would take some doing to make him down a second.

Ridge shrugged his shoulders into his coat and put on his hat.

"All right then, I'm on my way. Where is that hound? I don't want him announcing me to every Federal militiaman in Ray County."

"Earl's in the cellar," Pa said. "He won't bother you."

"Well, good-bye and good luck to you." The little doctor shook Pa's hand, then Frank's. When he came to me he took both my hands in his dimpled baby ones.

"I hope the boy makes it," he said. "I've known Jesse James since the day he entered this world. It was in the fall, as I recall, just about this time of year. He's a willful lad, with a bit of the devil in him, but likable all the same." He leaned in close and dropped his voice to a whisper as though we were fellow conspirators. "You'll take good care of him, Miss Rood. I have no doubt of it."

And with that he was out the door, stealing away from the house like a midnight robber. I watched till he vanished into the trees, wondering what he meant by that last and why his words made me blush. But, for whatever the reason, Doc was right about me because I stayed by Jesse's side almost constantly for the next two days, changing his bandages, sponging his head and shoulders with cool well water, slipping the bitter quinine in his drink every hour. Thirsty as he was, he gulped it down, though he wrinkled his nose and made a face like something smelled bad afterwards. When his fever was at its peak he ranted, talking to his mother and brother and sometimes to a girl named Sue. I found myself hoping this Sue was a sister and not a sweetheart.

On the morning of the third day, I found Jess awake and alert, asking for water. There was a life in his blue eyes I hadn't seen for some time.

"Was Doc Ridge here?" he said. "Or did I dream it?"

"He was here," I said. "Frank's been too, a couple times."

"Anyone else?"

Who was he expecting? Sue maybe?

"Just those two wastrels Bill Anderson sent," I said. "Nat and Ol, good-for-nothings, the pair of them. Ol eats like a field hand and Nat sits on the porch all day watching the road like he expects trouble."

Jesse nodded.

"Oliver's all right. We've known him a long time, me and Frank. Nat Tigue ain't mannerly, I grant you, but he's a good one to have on your side in a fight. You can believe that."

Better with you than against you, I reckoned that was so.

"Can you eat?" I said. "I'm about to fix breakfast. You should take some."

"Yes," he said, smiling the first full smile I'd seen from him in some time. "I believe I could."

Despite my lack of sleep I went about my kitchen work that morning with a full and happy heart. The rosy sunrise outside the window matched my mood; for the first time in a long while the coming day held promise and not just hours to fill up. Nothing, not Ol's wet snores from the parlor or the sight of Nat emerging from the privy buttoning his trousers, diminished my high feeling.

I wanted to make something especially tasty in celebration of Jesse's recovery, so I fried up the last of our Maplewood-cured ham, scrambled eggs, sliced our reddest tomatoes, and fixed oatmeal too—giving Jess all the raisins, extra sugar, and cream in his bowl instead of milk. After, I worried the cream might prove too rich for his depleted body, but he suffered no misadventure.

The day came cool and windy, mostly overcast, though every now and then a fugitive shaft of sunshine broke through. Today was Tuesday, wash day, and a heavy day of work for me since I was laundering for six now. It took up the whole morning. First I had to build a fire big enough to heat two kettles of water—soft rainwater if I had it and well water if I didn't—one for whites and another for coloreds and britches.

While the water heated I made starch out of flour and water and when the water was boiling I shaved a whole cake of lye soap into the whites kettle and a soft, sweeter soap for the delicates and coloreds. Then I stirred the things with a long battling stick, scrubbed the hot, wet britches on a board, rinsed and blued and starched, then hung the damn heavy things to dry on the line Pa strung between two dogwoods in the kitchen yard. By the time I finished my hands were red and scalded and wrinkled as the raisins in Jesse's oatmeal. With the leftover soapy water I scrubbed the front porch, and the rinse I emptied onto Ma's flower garden even though it didn't have any flowers in it anymore.

I learned how to do all this from watching Jerusha, the black woman who used to live with us, who'd been with us since before I was born. A slave, I guess you'd call her, though none of us thought of Jerusha that way. She was just a part of the family, a comfortable part. Leastways, the boys and I felt that about her, I don't know how it was with Pa and Ma. How many times I watched her launder our clothes in the kitchen yard on warm days, in the barn on cold or rainy ones. I started helping out when I got old enough because I liked the smell of the soaps and the African songs she sang as she worked the paddle. We were laundering that sunny fall morning when Doc Jennison and his scaly Kansas Jayhawkers came to plunder.

"Woman!" Jennison shouted at her like he was the great emancipator himself. "Are you ready for your freedom?"

When she hesitated he went all red in the face and shouted even louder.

"I said are you ready to cast off your shackles? Are you ready to drink the sweet and heady wine of freedom?"

When still she said nothing he ordered two of his boys to pick her up and put her in our wagon, which the Jayhawkers were already piling high with our belongings. I stood in the yard by the steaming kettles, my mouth open, and when the bluebellies came for Jerusha I turned and ran to the house taking a coward's refuge in my room. This memory shames me now. I know now the Lord hates a coward. I should've run for Pa's shotgun instead.

I watched from my bedroom window as Jennison asked Jerusha if she had any blankets or bedclothes or anything else she wished to take. He was a scrawny, red-headed man who may or may not have been a trained doctor but was for sure a thief, cutthroat, and scoundrel of the first water.

She continued mute but he waved his hand dismissively. "No matter," he said. "We'll do your packing for you. Pony, round up the mistress's things. Clothes, jewelry, silver, any pretty thing that catches your eye and be quick about it!"

Jerusha got to her feet in the wagon and raised her fist.

"Don't you take those things!" she cried. "Those are meant for Hattie. Don't you steal from her!"

I was frightened for all of us, for Jerusha, who would have to leave with Jennison and his Kansas trash no matter what she wanted, and especially for Pa who'd been caught out in the open in the field and stood beside the barn with one of those devils holding a gun to his side.

"Shut your mouth, woman!" Jennison bellowed. "Pony, get to it! Go in that house and take all you can carry."

I heard the Jayhawker's heavy boots on the parlor floor, the sound of drawers opening and crashing to the floor, his footfalls on the stairs. I thought about fleeing to the loft but did not for fear they would torch the house and I would be burned alive. Any death but a fiery one!

The Jayhawker, Pony, stopped outside my door and stared in at me. He was young, about nineteen or so, with a harelip that made his speech difficult to understand.

"Ahm takin' the silver," he said, raising a feed bag heavy with my dowry inheritance. "Ahm takin' it 'cause Doc said to an' ah don' wan' no truck with him neither. Ah did'n take the jewry ah foun', them earbobs an' the cameo. Ah lef 'em for you."

Was I supposed to thank him? I was not inclined that way. He started down the stairs with his loot, then turned back to me.

"Ahm sorry. Ah wish none of this was happnin'," he said. "Ah wish ah was home with my Ma, eatin' apple pie in the kitchen."

We never saw or heard of Jerusha again. Not a day passes I don't wonder what became of her.

This was what I remembered as I stirred the wash above the fire.

Chapter Six

I was lucky with the weather; the rain held off till the clothes were nearly dry. The first drops started falling as I took them down. Lazy Ol surprised me by holding my basket, but Nat maintained his silent vigil on the porch. There he sat, hour after hour, day after day, carving on his bit of wood, watching and waiting. Whatever or whoever it was he expected, I was in no hurry to find out.

Pa and Cy stayed out in the field despite the rain. We hadn't had much of that this summer and Pa struggled to make the most of what little crop he managed to coax up out of the soil. This rain this day was a good one, the soft, soaking kind, the kind Jerusha used to call a "female" rain. The "male" ones were the noisy, blowy, bothersome sort. She used to tell me and Ben and Doak stories about how it was in the olden days back in Africa, back before her granddaddy was caught by slavers, when animals talked and spirits roamed the shadow world behind this one. Her stories were funny and scary and so strong you couldn't stop thinking of them for days afterward. I never got my fill of them. Truth be told, I liked her stories a heck of a lot better than the Bible ones Ma used to read to us on Sunday mornings. Ma's God did not seem to have a drop of humor or charity in him.

Looking back, I guess you could say Jerusha's stories taught me a lot about the world and the overall fitness of things. They helped me understand how big and strange the world is, how much there is to see and touch and taste and smell, and I wanted my share. I wanted more from life than the normal girly things like poonah work and painting flowers on porcelain vases and reading Bible stories. I did not want to spend my days trapped indoors cooking and cleaning and washing and sewing. No, I wanted a life rich with adventure and reward, a Montana life, a life big as a man's. This war was interfering with my plans in all manner of ways.

After putting the laundry away I took a plate of cookies up to Jesse. I spent more time in the loft than I needed to but I liked being with him. He felt the same; I could tell by the way his face lit up when he saw me. That smile was double-nice when he saw the cookies.

"You like molasses jumbles?" I said, settling on the floor next to his cot. For a change it was nice up there, cool, with the rain pattering on the roof above us.

"Well I guess I do!"

As he reached for a cookie I noticed again the damaged finger on his left hand. I asked him what happened. To my surprise, he was bashful about it, taking the jumble with his right hand and sticking the other under the blanket.

"I don't like people looking at it," he said.

It wasn't polite, but I laughed. I couldn't help it.

"Why, Jesse, that hole in your chest is worse to look at by far! So, what was it then? You shoot yourself on accident?"

I could tell by his face that I'd hit the nail on the head.

"It happened while I was cleaning a gun. But that was a long time ago, before I knew how to handle a gun."

This was a fat opportunity and I could not resist it.

"So now I suppose you are expert in the use of firearms?" I said. "Equal to Billy Quantrill himself, are you?"

I expected this to bring out the rooster in him like it would my brothers and other boys I've known, but instead he grinned at me, like he saw the humor in himself. He was a live one, this Jesse James. I liked him very much.

"I'll tell you something." He pulled his maimed hand from under the blanket and held the finger aloft for my inspection. "I told the Lord I would never take His name in vain and I did not do it then, when I shot off my finger, even though it hurt like the devil."

If this was true, I thought, then Jesse had a will of iron.

"Why did you make that vow?" I said.

"It was a private matter, between me and Him. He held up His end so now I'll hold mine. Anyhow, according to my brother and others who was there, I said something like 'dodd-dingus pistol.' I don't remember it myself. That's why Buck and them call me Dingus."

I had wondered about it.

"As for the other, no, I ain't Quantrill's equal yet, but I will be someday. I ain't as green as you think, Hattie Rood. I've seen the elephant, don't think I haven't."

An unwelcome thought came to me.

"You weren't in on that Lawrence business were you?"

This was a sore point with me, not only because it involved the murder of innocents but because it brought the wrath of the Federal government down on the people like me and Pa. To punish bushwhackers and the families who gave them succor, General Tom Ewing, who was Tecumseh Sherman's brother-in-law and Lucifer in a blue uniform, ordered the evacuation of four counties. General Orders No. 11 made thousands of western Missourians refugees in their own homeland with nothing but the clothes on their backs and what little would fit in a wheelbarrow. A good many of those needful souls drifted into Ray County, shining the light of suspicion on us and draining the well faster when it was already near dry. Way I saw it, Quantrill's Lawrence action brought nothing but woe.

"Frank was there but I wasn't," Jesse said, unaware of my strong opinion. "I would've gone but Quantrill wouldn't have me. Said I was too young. He let me load pistols for him and the boys, though—that's when the finger business happened."

I asked him when he took to the bush.

"This spring," he said. "It was Fletch Taylor came through Clay County recruiting for Bill Anderson's company of guerillas. You know Fletch Taylor?"

I did not know him personal but I knew of him. Everybody in west Missouri knew of Taylor, one of Quantrill's original lieutenants. Although tiny in stature, Taylor was said to be long on vengeance. Misfortune visited any man who ran afoul of him. Rumor had it that he and Quantrill had a falling out in the spring. Likely Taylor was one of those former confederates Quantrill was on the lookout for that day he and Kate came to our farm.

"Anderson puts great stock in us Clay County boys," Jesse said with pride. "He says we're the best fighters he's got!"

Now everyone knows a healing man should not be inflamed, that he should avoid all but the most Christian passions, but Bill Anderson was a scalp taker, an ear cutter, and despoiler of black women, and I could not countenance this prideful mention of his name without making my feelings known.

"You ought not ride with that devil," I said. "You'll find no glory in it."

"Glory?" Jesse laughed. "This ain't about glory, Hattie—it's about justice! Eye for an eye, tooth for a tooth. It's about making them Yankees and Jayhawkers pay for what they done to us, the people of Missouri."

He was getting exercised so I let it go. I was trying to think up a new line of conversation when a voice hailed from outside.

"Hello the house!"

I crawled to the porthole window. It was Joe Craighead, standing in his wagon holding the reins of his two-horse team in one hand and shielding his eyes from the blowing rain with the other.

"Who's that?" Jesse tried to sit. "Where's Ol and Nat?"

I wondered the same as I pushed him back on the cot.

"Don't worry. He's no trouble for you. It's just Joe—a boy I know. A Southern boy."

He raised his eyebrows suggestively and I felt my face go red.

"He's not my sweetheart," I said quickly, though of course he was, or was meant to be. "I've got to go, though."

I started down the ladder but Jesse stopped me.

"Hattie."

He propped himself up on one elbow. His face was serious in the gray light.

"Don't tell Joe about us," he said. "Don't, for his sake."

Chapter Seven

I waited for Joe on the porch as he urged his team forward. The wagon was loaded though with what I could not tell, as the bed was covered with a canvas tarpaulin. Joe jumped down and joined me on the porch, pulling his rubber poncho over his head. Despite that outer garment his clothes were wet through and dripping, leaving puddles on the white-painted floorboards.

"I don't know why I bother with this thing," he said. "It's hot as the dickens and no good anyhow." He ran his hands through his blond hair, trying to smooth it down, but it was thick and cowlicky and stood straight up at the crown and forehead, making him look younger than his eighteen years.

"It sure is good to see you, Hattie. I've been awful worried ever since I heard you took the fever."

Joe was tall and strong and without question the most sought-after boy in Ray County. This was due to the fact that he was handsome and kind, his father owned the dry goods store in Richmond and also there weren't many able-bodied young men around to give him competition. To his credit, Joe was not proud of his availability. He would rather be with Doak and them, fighting with General Sterling Price, but Joe's father would not allow it on account of Joe's older brother fell at Pea Ridge in February of '62 and the old man could not countenance the prospect of losing his only surviving child.

No one around here held this against him, or Joe for that matter. Everybody loved Joe—and me, I loved him too, just not that way. More like a brother. Just thinking about doing the thing with him seemed flat-out indecent. More and more I was coming to realize I could not be Joe's wife, though I hadn't worked up the nerve to say it yet.

"I'm all right, Joe," I said. Over his shoulder I saw Nat stepping around the side of the barn with his pistol in hand. He caught my eye and drew the barrel of his gun across his throat like it was a knife blade. My heart banged against my ribs like a wasp trapped in a bottle. Nat had killed many men, I was sure. One more wouldn't matter much.

"You look good." Joe smiled, unaware that death stood behind him. "Too skinny but pretty as ever! Since you ain't been to town for a while I brought you and your Pa some groceries. Thought you might be short."

I took Joe's arm and led him into the house. All the while I felt Nat's eyes on us, and my skin tingled as I imagined a slug tearing into Joe's broad back. I pulled him close hoping with no good reason that Nat wouldn't risk hitting me. Joe was happily surprised by this unusually warm reception.

"Why, Hattie, if I'd known you'd be so glad to see me, I'd have come sooner."

I stole a quick backward look over my shoulder as I closed the door. Nat had disappeared.

"Come into the kitchen, Joe," I said. "I'll fix you something."

He settled in at the table and I gave him coffee and a piece of Journey Cake, a recipe my grandmother brought with her from old Kentucky a half century before. It was a good company treat and easy to keep because it was made from cornmeal, buttermilk, and molasses—no eggs—and we wrapped it in a whiskey-soaked cheesecloth so it stayed nice and moist.

"I came out here straight off when I heard you were sick, but your Pa said you couldn't have visitors, doctor's orders,"

Joe said. "Did he tell you?"

"He told me," I said. "We didn't know if it was catching."

I set another thick slice of cake on the table. As Joe ate I went to the window. No sign of Nat and Ol.

"Hattie? Will you?"

Joe had been talking all this time but I hadn't heard a word.

"Will I what?" I said.

"Come riding on Sunday?"

I didn't want Joe coming back here; I was afraid of what might happen and I didn't want to go riding anyhow. I was needed here. Jesse would need me.

"I don't know, Joe," I said. "It's not a good idea. The woods are full of men who'd shoot you and me both for a good horse. You know that."

He got up from the table and came to me, taking my hand in his big, calloused paw.

"Nobody's going to hurt you, Hattie," he said. "They'd have to get by me first."

The heat in his eyes unnerved me. I tried to pull my hand away but Joe wouldn't let it go. I knew then he had come out here not only to bring groceries but to have his say.

"I have feelings for you, Hat," he said. The gray light from the window fell sideways across his face showing the stubble of his blond beard. "I always have. You remember that day we found the Injun grave by the river?"

Yes, I remembered the warm fall afternoon when the four of us—me, my brothers, and Joe—uncovered an ancient, soil-stained skeleton and cache of afterlife treasures. We found pipes of red pipestone, arrow points made from iron and stone, knife blades, smooth slabs of hematite, used for I don't know what, and, curiously, the bent and lensless frames of a white man's eyeglasses. Even then, in the wild excitement of discovery, I sensed Joe's regard for me. That was the first time I saw him looking at me in a way that was amorous and adult-like. I didn't like it.

He continued: "That's when I knew I'd marry you, Hattie, that day. I think about you all the time, I do, and when I heard you were sick I nearly went crazy! If anything happened to you...well...maybe it's time we..."

At that moment Pa came through the kitchen door, and I was so relieved to see him I could have kissed his face. Instead I jumped to the stove to pour him a cup of coffee, catching a glimpse of Joe's disappointment as I did so. Oh, I wished Joe would leave so I could go up to the loft, to Jesse!

"Joe!" Pa smiled with true affection and stuck out his hand. "Is that your wagon out front?"

Pa looked so old and frail standing next to Joe it gave me a shock. Was Pa declining? Was he sick or did he appear so simply because Joe was so strong? I tried to picture Pa as a stout, robust young man and could not feature it. Long as I could remember he was tired and careworn, but not so much as now.

"How you been keepin', Captain?" Joe said. "Will you have any tobacco this year?"

That was a question I, myself, was curious about as Pa did not discuss such matters with me, a daughter. I had my doubts. Tobacco was a needy weed that took a toll on its grower—enslaved him, you might say. It started in the spring when sprouting plants were transplanted from seedbeds to the field. Careful tending was required all through the summer until the cutting and the curing in the fall, and it was backbreaking toil, with many pitfalls along the way. If a man was not properly attentive with his shovel, plow, and hoe early-on, cutworms would devour the roots. If the leaf was cut before it was properly ripe, a bitter, chaffy product would result. Pa and Cy worked like mules, but they were only two men and still learning this form of husbandry.

"Some," Pa said. "We'll get by, God willing."

Of course the will was less God's than Bill Anderson's. Even if Pa's crop was adequate, all depended on whether the river was open, whether Anderson's bushwhackers would let the steamboats and barges pass downriver to St. Louis. If not, if they continued their current practice of firing on passing boats, halting all traffic and commerce, Pa's crop would rot in the Camden stemmery along with everyone else's.

Joe shot me a quick look before continuing.

"Times are hard, Captain, hard for all of us. I know I've said this before, but you and Hattie ought to move to town for a while. You could keep your fields going, you and Cy could work days, then stay with us nights. You're not safe out here alone, not with things like they are nowadays. Come to town, why don't you, just till it settles down? Pa and me, we've got room. Heck, we've got more than we need. We rattle around in that big house." Here his sun-darkened face pinked up some. "We'd welcome the company."

He meant mine in particular. Joe's mother died long ago and the Craighead house was sorely in need of a woman's touch.

Pa shook his head. Him and Joe had been down this road more than once.

"It's a generous offer, Joe, but this is our home. I can't leave it. I guess we'll stay."

"Well, suit yourself," Joe said. "I brought groceries—vegetables and flour, oil for the lamps. I figured you'd need it. Now the rain's stopped, I'll start unloading."

Anxious about Nat and Ol, I checked the window again, looking to the barn. I was relieved not to see them.

"I can't pay you for it, Joe," Pa said. "Not now anyhow. Maybe not for a while."

Maybe never, I thought. But Joe waved his hand like he was brushing off a fly.

"It don't matter, Captain," he said. "Where do you want these things, Hattie?"

I showed Joe which of the barrels and bags went to the pantry and which to the underground cellar. In the autumn of a good year, the cellar would hold bins full of apples and potatoes, turnips and carrots, barrels of pork and corned beef, food enough to see us through the winter and six weeks' time of want that came every spring when the kept foods were gone and the fresh ones not ripe for eating. But this was not a good autumn and our cellar was near empty, a clean space of whitewashed brick floor and bare walls. I was embarrassed by our poverty, but Joe kept up a cheerful chatter like he did not notice.

Though Nat and Ol stayed away, I was nervous as a cat the whole time, never knowing when they would show their scaly faces. When the unloading was done, Joe rightly expected an invitation to dinner. I was ashamed not to offer one, but I hustled him back to Richmond anyhow. He didn't know it was for his own good and my bad manners stung him. One day I would explain it to him, but at present a man's life was cheap in Missouri and I didn't want Joe's to be the next one sold for a whistle.

I walked him out to his wagon. He had a long face when he climbed up and took his seat.

"Did I upset you with what I said before, you know, in the kitchen?" He looked down at me with a puzzled smile. "Is that why you're rushing me off?"

The rain held off though the sky was dark and lowering. Thunder rumbled and wind ruffled the treetops.

"No, Joe. I just don't want you caught in the storm is all."

He sighed and picked up the reins.

"All right, Hattie. But I'll be back Sunday for our ride. Don't forget."

He slapped the reins down on the horses' backs and turned the team. I watched till he reached the river road, where he rounded the bend with a final wave of his hand. Nat watched, too, from the corner of the house.

"I thought that Dutchman wouldn't never leave," he said. "It got dull, sittin' in the barn with only Ol's ugly mug to look at."

"Joe's not a Dutchman," I said. "He's American, same as you and me. Southern, too."

Nat spat, arcing a tobacco-brown glob that landed plop at my feet.

"He looks like a Dutchy," he said.

"Didn't your mother ever tell you you can't judge a man by the look of him?"

He favored me with one of his yellow smiles.

"Don't you go worryin' yourself about what my mother taught me. But if you're interested in what I know, I'll be glad to show you a few things."

I didn't like this turn in the conversation and started back toward the house. Nat put himself between me and the door.

"Did you tell that square-head about us? Did he see anything?"

"No. To both."

Nat smiled again, sly-like, as if him and me shared a secret.

"No, I guess he didn't. That boy don't see much when you're around. Can't say I blame him, neither."

He stepped in closer.

"I'd like us to get better acquainted, but then, if you're used to chuckle-heads like that Dutchman," he moved his head in Joe's direction, "you wouldn't know how to handle a man in full, which is what I am."

Ol appeared then at the corner of the house. His grin told me he'd been listening.

"I know how to handle a jackass, Nat Tigue," I said. "Which is what you are."

Nat's smile evaporated, but Ol's laughter followed me into the house.

Chapter Eight

I was late getting dinner and it was full dark by the time I took Jesse his plate. I knew something was wrong the moment I stuck my head through the loft door. The candle by his cot wasn't lit like usual and his breathing sounded different, wet and rattly.

I lit the candle. Even its feeble light was enough to show me Jesse was in trouble. I held the candle close to his face, feeling a hot surge of panic. His skin was blanched, the color of oatmeal. Even his lips were bloodless and pale. What could have happened? He was doing so well just a few hours before!

"Jesse," I said, "Jess. Can you hear me?"

His eyelids fluttered. His lashes were black and long as a girl's.

"Ma? Is that you?"

"No, Jess, it's me. Hattie. What's wrong? What do you feel?"

"Are the boys back, Ma? Is Buck home?"

I touched his forehead. It was dry and hot as a stone in the sun. Having taken no vow like Jesse's, I swore out loud, cursing my helplessness. How could I help him? What should I do? My eyes burned with tears, as much for myself as for him. Why had this terrible thing happened and why had the responsibility of saving him landed on me? How unfair, how cruel it all was! If he died I would blame myself forever, I knew this. If deprived of him, would I ever find another who inspired the same feeling in me? Would I spend the rest of my days pining for this blue-eyed boy? I wallowed in self-pity for a time, then Mother Reality came along and shook me by the shoulders as she did anytime I started to lament my lot. Unfair or not, Henrietta Rood, you are all Jesse's got so get busy!

Thunder rolled in the west and a gust from the window guttered the candle. More rain was coming. This much was good as it would cool the air and keep it moving through the loft. Still, the night would be a long one.

First order of business was to figure out some way to get Doc Ridge back here. Maybe Nat and Ol, the twin rapscallions, could actually make themselves useful for a change!

I crawled to the window and called down to Nat on the porch.

"Come up here! Hurry!"

Lamplight danced on the sloping ceiling as Nat climbed the ladder. With a grunt he heaved himself through the opening and joined me at the bedside. He gave Jesse the fisheye.

"He don't look so good." He put his lantern on the floor beside me and leaned in for a closer inspection. "What's the problem now? I thought he was getting better."

"He was. I don't know what this is. Might be lung fever but I'm no expert."

I pressed my hand to Jesse's chest. His heart was racing as I knew it would be.

"We need that doctor back here," I said. "Doc Ridge. You need to go get him."

"Me? I don't know how to find that fat little sawbones and even if I did it probably wouldn't do no good. Look at him—he's white as a ghost!"

A red rage flamed up inside me and I hopped up on my feet, nearly banging my head on the rafters. Could any creature on God's green earth possibly be more worthless than this damned Nat Tigue!

"Well go find Frank then!" I said. "You can do that, can't you? Find Frank and tell him Jesse needs that doctor. Do it right now this very instant!" I stamped my foot on the floor so hard the beans bounced off Jesse's plate.

Nat gave me a look like he would rip my head off and spit down the hole. We glared at each other for a time, me and him, then Nat gave in, though it clearly pained him to do it.

"I'll go for Buck." He spoke in a tight voice as he bent to pick up the lantern. "I will, but not because you said so. I'm doing it because Bill Anderson is partial to our friend Dingus here and my orders are to look out for the son-of-a-bitch."

He started down the ladder then stopped, his glittering black eyes fixed on me in the candlelight. There was no love lost between me and Nat Tigue, sure enough.

"If I was you, girl, I'd watch that mouth. You keep on popping off like that and somebody's gonna teach you some manners. And it will be a mighty hard lesson."

Chapter Nine

I stayed by Jesse's side sponging his forehead with a cloth, trying to cool him down but not succeeding. The fever burned like a furnace inside him. Was he dying? I took no solace in the notion he might be entering a better world. I was raised on the Bible and taught to be a prayerful Christian girl but in truth I had serious doubts about much of it, particularly the heavenly afterlife. Much as I wanted to believe, I did not, not truly, and I didn't see how lying about it would do any good.

For lack of anything else to do I changed his bandages and cleaned his wound, but this time I got no warming smile for my efforts. Jesse never woke up though he did mutter words I could not make out. His breath came fast and shallow like he was running a foot race. To make things worse, he started up with a cough, not much at first but then hard and racking. Every spell shook him so, I feared he'd bust himself open again.

Time passed like a broken clock. I had to go about my usual business, yet I went like a sleepwalker, milking Eugenie at dawn, fixing meals, making soap, cleaning floors. Throughout the day I made many trips to the loft, finding Jesse unchanged—sleeping feverishly, occasionally seized with a coughing fit.

Nat had not returned by supper time. I set the table with bacon and green beans from our garden, cornbread, and tomatoes, but I had no appetite myself. I moved around the kitchen, listening in as Pa, Cy, and Ol discussed the war, how Lady Fortune was smiling on Black Abe's army and showing us Southern folks her backside. It wasn't just, there was no justice to it, but Tecumseh Sherman and his bummers were laying waste to Georgia unimpeded and it appeared that Atlanta soon would fall if it hadn't already. In the contrary way that seems to mark us, these portents of ruin only made our Missouri boys fight all the harder.

In recent developments Jennison's Jayhawkers had joined up with Colonel James Ford and his Colorado mountain hogs and together these vandals set about terrorizing the western part of the state, pillaging, murdering, and putting the torch to anything that would take a flame. Despite the sweltering mid-August heat that bore down on the bodies of man and beast like a wet blanket of heavy wool, our boys fought two bloody battles that month, one near the town of Fredericksburg on the Ray County line and another in the county of Platte. After this second, Platte City had only nineteen quick menfolk remaining, the rest having been killed or run off.

But never you mind all that, Ol said, because the tide was fixing to turn. In just a few weeks old Pap and his army would boil up from Arkansas to free Missouri of the Yankee oppressor.

"Yessir." Ol nodded his shaggy head in a knowing fashion. "Sterling Price is on the march, or will be soon enough. Then us boys riding with Anderson and Taylor and Todd and Thrailkill—we will throw in with him and we will show them bluebelly bastards who the real pukes are!"

I don't know why the Yanks called us Missourians pukes but I knew I didn't like it. No one did.

Me, I took Ol's proclamations with a grain of salt. Talk of Sterling Price's return to Missouri had been on the air for some time. Maybe it was true, but even so I was of two minds about it. Doak was with Price and I longed to see him again. We hadn't had a letter for some time and I was beginning to fear the worst. Pa was too, but he would not say so because of superstition. On August 13, 1861, Pa said he had a bad feeling about my older brother, Ben, and we received news of his death within the hour.

So, much as I wanted to see Doak, another part of me hoped Price would stay away. If he came north he would draw Federal troops down on us like flies on a cowpie. Also, truth to tell, I had no great faith in the old man's soldiering skills. Well I remembered the first time I saw him, when his army, fresh from victory at Wilson's Creek, took Lexington, a port town on the south bank of the Missouri River. That was the day Doak went for a soldier, even though Ben was new to his grave and even though me and Pa begged him not to. Well, I begged. Pa asked. But Doak was fixed on it, even more because of Ben, and Pa said he had to respect that. I went to Lexington with Doak and we rode double on Kitturah, our sorrel palfrey. I went because I needed to see him off, plus Kitt was the only horse we had left and I would have to ride her back home.

"There he is," Doak said as we rode into town. He pointed to a fat, red-faced man on horseback reviewing a ragged line of recruits. "Old Pap himself, the savior of Missouri."

I had expected a fine military fellow in uniform, a Missouri version of General Robert Lee. Instead I saw an old man in a grimy white suit who looked not like a general but an aging gentleman-planter fallen on hard times. None of his soldiers had uniforms, not even the officers who made themselves known by tying strips of colored cloth to their shirts to mark their rank.

Price and his boys looked like a ragtag outfit to me, although I didn't say so as Doak was feeling manly and full of himself. My lack of confidence proved out later that very month when the Union General John Fremont marched west from St. Louis and without even popping a sweat drove Price and his army not only out of Lexington but clean out of Missouri and down into Arkansas. For certain, Old Pap was no Robert Lee.

Ol yammered on about the coming invasion, but I'd heard enough. I went to the loft with clean linens for Jesse's bed. By now I'd become expert at changing his cot with him in it. I did this smoothly, without disturbing him or prompting a violent coughing fit.

That night I did not go to my room as usual but stretched out on the floor to pass the night beside him. He was so low I could not leave him; I feared he would slip away without me there to pull him back. I lay awake for some time, my hand on the cot touching his body so I could feel him breathing, listening to the croak of the bullfrogs and the buzz of the cicadas down by the river.

Chapter Ten

Frank and Nat came at dawn, announced by Earl's excited barking. To my dismay they came alone, without the little doctor. I stuck my head out the window and called down to them.

"Where is he? Where's Doc Ridge?"

Remembering his first visit, I scanned the dark woods that lined the river road, hoping to see him running from the trees, but I didn't.

"He ain't coming," Frank said. Wearily he slid from the saddle and tied his horse to the porch rail. "He's afraid the Feds will find out he's treating a Secesh and string him up. He won't chance it."

Nat snorted. "The little turd showed the white feather. No surprise there. Not to me."

He dropped to the ground and out of meanness swung a boot at Earl, who easily avoided injury.

Frank joined me in the loft.

"How is he?" he said, studying his brother in the red morning light. "Any better?"

Frank's naturally long face was stretched even longer with tiredness and worry. Though he was but four years older, Frank looked old enough just then to be Jesse's granddaddy.

"He had a bad night. He's still fevering and he's got a hard cough. I am heartily sorry Doc Ridge didn't come back with you." I cleared my throat to hide the tremble in my voice.

Jesse did not stir, apparently unaware of our voices. His illness thinned him, sharpening his cheekbones and deepening the set of his eyes. Still, he was the most beautiful boy—to my eyes, grown more so by the prospect of loss.

Frank rubbed a dirty hand across his eyes.

"It's hard to see Jess so low," he said. "I blame myself for it. He looks up to me, always has. He's wanted to ride with me ever since I started bringing the boys round to the farm. It's my fault he's here."

"You ain't so much, Buck." Jesse's eyes opened and he smiled. "I took to the bush to get away from Ma is what."

Frank squatted by the cot and took Jesse's left hand.

"Hello, brother. How do you feel?"

"Tip top. Splendid."

Frank shook his head. "I'll tell you true, Dingus, this malingering of yours is giving me and this pretty girl here a sharp pain in the backside."

"I don't doubt it."

Jesse coughed, a hard seizure that left him gasping.

"Where's Doc Ridge?" he said when it passed.

"That worthless son-of-a-bitch," Frank said. "He wouldn't come with me. Said it was too dangerous. He'll pay for that someday."

"Oh well," Jesse said. "It probably don't matter anyhow. I feel done for."

I kneeled beside him with a cup of water and lifted his head. His hair was wet in my hand.

"Boo hoo," I said, pretending a light heart though my own was heavy as lead. "Quit feeling sorry for yourself. You ain't so bad. I seen worse."

He took a few sips, thanking me with his eyes. Every time I looked into them I had the sensation of falling into their bottomless blue depths.

"You sure are sweet, Hattie," he said. "You sure are a sweet girl."

I felt a clutch in my throat and swallowed it down. Do not cry, Henrietta Rood, I said to myself. Don't you be a ninny in front of him.

Frank came to my rescue, asking me to leave him and Jesse alone for a few minutes. I went to the kitchen and sat at the table with my head in my hands. There was breakfast to get but I was too tired, too tired even to light the candle. I sat in the dark like a person made of stone. Once I took pride in this tidy kitchen with its neatly whitewashed walls and new-painted floor and the clean dishcloths hanging on nails in a row above the sink. Now, I didn't care about any of it. My world and everything in it was of no account and deserving of pity.

I sat there till I heard boots on the stairs. Frank and Ol came in and sat at the table across from me.

"Why you sittin' in the dark?" Ol said. He popped a wooden match to flame with his thumbnail and lit the candle.

I didn't answer.

"Doc Ridge said Jesse's symptoms sound like pneumonia," Frank said. "Someone needs to stay right by him every minute till the crisis comes. Will you do that, Hattie? Will you stay with him?"

I nodded. I'd seen a lung crisis before. It was a terrible thing to behold, but I watched my auntie get cousin Sal through it and I reckon I could do the same for Jess. Frank continued:

"You need to thump him on the chest from time to time to keep the phlegm loose and turn him too, so it doesn't sink to one place and stick. He said to cover his chest with a mustard plaster and leave the window open all the time so the air stays pure. And be sure to keep his bed and room clean with soap and water."

I was doing all that already, everything but the mustard plaster.

"Also he will require medicine, Doc said. Calomel."

"And I don't suppose he gave you any of that?" I said.

"He didn't. Said it's hard to come by. Can you get some?"

I thought of Joe. His father sold apothecary items at his mercantile. Though I shrank at the thought of taking advantage of Joe's tender regard for me, I would do it if it meant saving Jesse's life.

"I might," I said.

Frank leaned in and covered my hand with his.

"Jesse's right about you, Hattie, you are a sweet girl. Very sweet. We'll make it up to you some day, Jesse and I."

Ol, who had been silent till now, let out a loud hoot.

"Dammit Frank, that kid brother of yours gets his hand up more skirts than a dressmaker! Why ever time I turn around he's got himself some new—"

Quick as a hiccup Frank lashed out and boxed Ol a hard one on the ear.

"Shut up, Ol." Turning to me, Frank said, "Don't mind him, Hattie. Ol Shepherd has a grown man's body with a baby's brain. He doesn't know his ass from his elbow."

Ol, rubbing his reddened right ear, clearly objected to this characterization but he kept his mouth shut.

"I'll stay with Jess today," Frank said. "You go to Richmond, Hattie. You get Jesse that medicine. That calomel."

Our eyes met over the candle and I saw Frank had a strong determination. He must have thought I needed convincing, judging from what he said next.

"You know, Jesse is a special kind of boy and one who's worth saving, and I don't say that just because he's my brother. I'll tell you something about him and maybe you'll see what I mean.

"Our father died when Jesse was three. He went out to California for some reason—I was never real clear about why—and he died out there. Jess doesn't hardly remember him. Anyhow, few years later our Ma married this fellow Simms, and he was one mean son-of-a-bitch, pardon my language. We hated that old man, Jesse and me, but the county skunked us of our inheritance and Ma needed the money. Well, not only was he mean to us but he beat her, beat her pretty bad. One day Jess, who wasn't but five or six at the time, caught him slapping her around and he went after Old Man Simms like he was a bear and Simms a fresh side of bacon." Frank smiled at the memory. "Kicking and biting and yelling cuss words I didn't even know about. Course, Jess got locked in the cellar with his nose broke for his trouble, but still it shows you the sand he's got."

"What happened to Old Man Simms?"

"He died of a fit a few months after. That was a happy day for us, Jesse and me."

"And I bet you Jess hasn't spoke a cuss word since," I said, remembering Jesse's account of his bargain with the Lord.

Frank looked surprised. "You may be right. I never thought about it."

"I'll go to Richmond this morning," I said. "I'll get the calomel."

My determination to save Jesse was as great as Frank's, but for a very different reason.

Chapter Eleven

Before leaving I covered Jesse's chest with a plaster made from Doc Ridge's recipe of dry mustard, water and wood ash from the stove. Then I put on my best dress—a black-and-white delaine with a snug-fitting bodice—and a cream-colored bonnet with straw flowers sewn into the sash. My shoes were the same tired brown lace-ups with the curled toes I wore every day; I had no choice.

Pa was surprised to see me so spruced up when he came to the kitchen for his breakfast.

"Why you dressed like that?" he said. "This ain't Sunday."

"I know it, Pa." I avoided his eyes as I set a plate of grits and pancakes on the table. "I'm going to town this morning." I said it not in the form of a question. "I'll need Kitt and the little wagon."

He poured a cup of coffee and sat down to the table, not saying a word. Cy came in and, sensing a tense situation, pulled out a chair and tucked into his food. I waited for what seemed an age till finally Pa was done eating.

"What do you want in town?" he said, pushing away his plate.

"Medicine for Jesse. He needs it."

"Says who?"

I told him about Frank's failed trip to Kansas City and Doc Ridge's diagnosis of pneumonia. I said I planned to get the medicine from Joe. At this Pa brought his hand down on the table so hard the dishes jumped.

"Maybe I don't give a damn what that boy needs! Maybe I'm more interested in what I need—what this family needs! That boy's not our blood, Hattie. I'm sorry he's hurt but we got to look out for ourselves!"

Pa's face was red and his neck veins stood out like strands of blue yarn. He wasn't finished.

"I'm sick of those good-for-nothing bushwhackers hanging around, looking for trouble, never doing a lick of work but eating like field hands! And I'm sick of that brother—Frank or Buck or whatever his name is—showing up at all hours, threatening to bring the Yankees down on us! It'll happen too—just you wait!"

After this outburst we sat in silence, the three of us: me, Pa and Cy. The rooster crowed out in the barnyard and I looked to the window, wishing myself out there with him. The morning sun was up, bringing a warm rosy glow, but its friendly light did not touch us in the kitchen.

"Captain Rood," Cy said. "You ought not to yell at Miss Hattie like that. Why, she's just trying to do her best for the boy is all."

This speech was out of character for Cy and Pa looked thunder at him. My blood was up too. I was going to Richmond if I had to walk every step of the way.

"That's so, Pa," I said. "You may repent it now, but it was you invited them in. It was you said Jesse could stay till he dies or gets better!"

While Pa could not argue the truth of this, he didn't like hearing it from me.

"All right," he said. "Let's say Craighead has this medicine. Just how do you intend to pay for it?" He raised his eyebrows. "Did the brother give you the money?"

That might be a problem. I had already given it some thought.

"I'll take it on credit," I said. "Joe trusts me."

Pa gave a short laugh. He was so red in the face I could almost believe, despite the hour, he had broken temperance. "Poor Joe!" he said. "Poor simple Joe. No doubt you're right. Joe Craighead would give you anything you asked for. Are you going to tell him about our guest? About the Clay County bushwhacker who's replaced him in your affections?"

Pa's anger was well beyond what I had anticipated. Did he fear for my safety? Or was he worried my actions would imperil Joe's feelings for me and therefore the money my marriage to a Craighead would bring us Roods?

Seeing I would not answer, Pa got to his feet and picked up his hat.

"I can't spare a day to drive you to Richmond," he said, never mind I hadn't asked him. "And I wouldn't anyhow. We've done enough for the boy. If he's so valuable to Bill Anderson let him come do for him. But if you're determined to go, there is something you can do for me. Post this letter."

He went to his room, returning with an envelope that he thrust at me. It was addressed to Doak Rood in Arkansas, care of General Sterling Price.

"By God, I wish my son was with me now," Pa said. Although he did not say "instead of this useless, troublesome girl," he may as well have. His meaning was clear enough. He left the kitchen, slamming the door behind him. Throughout all this ugliness Cy stayed at the table, staring down at his empty plate. Tears of hurt and anger burned my eyes. I squeezed them back but Cy saw.

"Aw, Hattie, the Captain ought not to talk to you like that," he said. "He wouldn't if things was normal, but he ain't himself these days."

I looked down at the letter, at Pa's childish handwriting, not trusting myself to look at Cy's wrinkled face, not trusting myself to speak. Cy got up from the table and walked to me, putting his hand on my shoulder. I kept my eyes on the floor, on his dirty brown boots. He patted my shoulder, then followed Pa out, closing the door softly behind him.

I stood like a statue, alone in the kitchen, feeling like a fool in my Sunday dress and bonnet. What a sorry girl I was! What a miserable, no-account creature! What chance of happiness was there for a skinny, red-haired Missouri girl like me, whose own Pa didn't even like her?

Then, as I always did when I was down at the mouth, I thought of Montana Territory, my private heaven. I thought of a place I read about in the newspaper called Last Chance Gulch, where gold lay on top of the ground just waiting for someone brave enough to go up there and pick it up. Me, I was brave enough. I might not be the prettiest girl in Missouri, or the smartest, but I had that steel in me. Jesse had it too. Yes, Last Chance Gulch, that was the place for Hattie Rood and Jesse James. Why should we spend our allotted earthly time in Ray County Missouri with the world going to smash all around us? We could do better! I'd tell him about Montana when he was well and he'd see the rightness of it too, I knew it.

Earl Smith scratched at the kitchen door and opening it I saw Kitturah in the barnyard finishing a nosebag of oats. Cy must have given her those. I could hitch her to the little wagon, an open buckboard with a long bed and built-up sides. I'd done it before.

"Come on, Earl," I said. "We're going to town."

I got Kitt into her harness and hitched to the wagon without dirtying my dress, then I packed a fast lunch of bread and cheese, wrapped it in paper, and tied it round with string. My heart beat fast as I walked to the wagon. I thought about Yankees and the free blacks and all the other freebooters who lived in the woods like old-time highwaymen. I thought of Pa. But most of all I thought about Jesse and what would happen if I didn't get his calomel. It was that kept me moving.

Earl and Kitt waited for me with solemn animal eyes that said, "Are you sure you want to do this?" I picked the dog up and dumped him in the back of the wagon where he landed with a whistling fart. The comicalness of this made me laugh and I felt better.

I climbed up on the bench and slapped the reins down on Kitt's bony back, raising little clouds of dust. She lurched into motion and we were under way. As we rolled down the drive I glanced over my shoulder to see Frank in the loft window. He waved and I waved back.

The morning was clouding up. It would be one of those August days when it stayed dawny-dark till nighttime. Earl Smith stood in the back of the wagon, scanning the roadside, his eyes barely clearing the sideboard. I started to relax a bit as we clopped along. Kitt's shoes marked a steady rhythm on the road. She moved slowly, like each foot weighed more than her knobby legs were made for. Soon we were halfway down the shady lane that would connect up with the turnpike to Richmond, some eight miles north and west.

"We'll be fine," I said aloud to Kitt and Earl. The dog smiled at me and Kitt's ears went up. "We will get that medicine and be home in time to make supper."

Earl turned back to his surveillance of the woods on either side of the road. It was about half past eight, I figured, no later. At this pace we should be in Richmond before noon. I raised my eyes again to the gray sky hanging over our heads like a low ceiling. Please, I prayed, don't let it rain. The road was hard as rock, but rain would turn it to mud in no time.

A cool wind rustled the flowers on my bonnet and raised gooseflesh on my skin. The woods were dark and quiet as the tomb. No birds, no buzzing insects, no quarrelsome housewife squirrels. The stillness served to heighten my nervousness; these woods usually boiled with life this time of year.

The sky got darker. To calm myself I hummed a tune, "What a Friend We Have in Jesus," but it occurred to me Jesus had not been such a friend lately and I quit it. Then I heard the sound of a horse coming up fast behind me, coming at the gallop, his hoofbeats loud as thunder in the dead woods. Earl Smith ran from one side of the wagon to the other, growling, hair bristling in a ridge between his bony shoulders.

"Hellfire Kitt!" I cursed and brought the reins down on her back. "Pick it up you old bonerack! Pick it up now!"

Kitturah moved a little faster, but there was no way the old horse would outrun whoever was coming up behind us. My mind raced. What to do, what to do? Though I had a ladies' pistol in my waist pocket, that little pop gun wouldn't do much damage unless I shot from good and close. Damn! I did not relish the thought of sending a bullet into human flesh and bone, but I would shoot a man in the face if it came to that. I would set aside my womanly softness, what little I had, if I had to.

I decided to affect a leisurely pace, like any country girl on her way to town. What choice did I have? Now I could hear the running horse's labored breaths. Kitt heard it too; her ears were up and forward and white showed in her eyes as she turned her head toward the sound.

Finally I worked up my courage and looked behind me. The rider was just beyond the bend in the road. I'd see him soon enough. I held my breath and waited, then laughed out loud when none other than old Cy came flying into view. He was riding one of Pa's plow mules without a saddle.

"Land o' Goshen, Cyrus!" I said when he reined up beside us. He and the mule were badly winded. "I thought Beelzebub himself was after me."

Cy dismounted and tied the mule's reins to a ringbolt on the back of the wagon.

"He may well be," he said, giving me a one-eyed glare as he climbed up on the bench and took the reins from my hands. "That's why I'm here. Your Pa will have my hide, but I could not work for worrying about you."

In truth I was glad to see him. Although Cy was old and thin as a shadow, he was a man and he carried a Navy revolver in his belt.

It was about noon and still overcast when we came to Richmond. Departing as we arrived were two columns of Union foot soldiers trudging along in their dusty wool coats, heads hanging. They were a sorry, beat-down lot, and barely took the trouble to look up as we rolled by. Their mounted officer gave us the once-over, though, and me in particular. He was a hatchet-faced, snaky-looking fellow and I was glad again of Cy's company.

On the outskirts of town we passed the stemmery, the livery stable and carriage shop, the gunsmith's and cooper's shops, the housepainting and wallpapering businesses, the Widow Lister's millinery establishment. The widow herself—a tall, handsome woman with a full-figure and a reputation for easy virtue, along with a good head for business—surprised me by giving Cy a flirty wave from the window. Doak once told me he thought Cy and the widow were friendly but I couldn't believe it. Guess it was true, though, because old Cy went red as a ripe tomato and would not look at me.

Craighead's Dry Goods was in the center of town, 'cross the square from the courthouse and jail. Noble Goe, Fouche Garner, and Branick Wilkerson—three wrinkled granddaddies who were so old they could talk about helping the sons of Daniel Boone clear the Boonslick road from St. Charles through to the salt licks of Howard County—sat nodding in chairs in front of the store while Joe labored on the boardwalk unloading hogsheads from a freighter. He was so strong he could lift a barrel single-handed, whereas two lesser men struggled with the same weight.

When he caught sight of us, he stopped and walked to our wagon, wiping his hands on his trousers.

"Hello, Hattie," he said with a wide smile. He reached out his hand to me, then thought better of it. "You look mighty pretty today, too pretty to touch my dirty hand. Hello, Cyrus. What brings you two to town?"

Joe's big grin tugged at my heart. He thought I fixed myself up pretty just for him and I guess in a way I did, only not the way he figured.

"We need something, Joe." I kept my voice low so as not to be heard by passersby. "Medicine. Can we talk somewhere private?"

His smile disappeared.

"Are you all right?" he said.

I nodded.

"Yes, me and Pa, we're fine. It's for someone else—no one you know. I don't want to talk here."

He lifted me down from the wagon, no longer worried about getting me dirty.

"Let's go inside," he said.

I left Cy with the wagon and followed Joe into the store. The interior was cool and dark with shelves reaching to the stamped tin ceiling on either side, and a long, waist-high counter running the length of the room. It smelled of crackers, sawdust, and peppermint. Harley Thomas, the clerk, was stocking canned goods and he turned to smile at us as we came in. Him and my brother Ben joined the State Guard together in June of '61. Most of Harley made it home but not all; one leg of his trousers was empty, pinned up at the hip.

"Afternoon, Hattie Rood." He was pale from the indoors work, but his smile was nice as ever. "How've you and the Captain been keeping? I heard you took the fever a while back."

"Hello Harley," I said. "Yes, I was down for a spell but I'm all right now. Pa's good too."

"What do you hear from Doak?"

That reminded me of Pa's letter keeping company with the pistol in my waist pocket.

"Nothing lately and it's got us worried."

Joe took me by the arm and guided me toward the rear of the store.

"Those calicos you want are in back, Hattie. I haven't even unpacked them yet. Harley, anyone comes in you're in charge."

Harley winked at me before turning back to his cans. Like everybody else he figured me and Joe were halfway to the altar. I followed Joe into the room he and Old Man Craighead used as an office. It was chock full of crates and barrels and bolts of colorful fabrics. In one corner stood an expensive-looking desk with a curved, roll-back top, and beside it a cast iron floor safe with Liberty Safe Co., Philadelphia, stenciled across the door in bold white letters.

When I started to tell Joe my tale of our need, he put a finger to his lips and drew the curtain that served as a door.

'There's bushwhackers at our house, Joe," I whispered. "Three of 'em, Bill Anderson's boys. One was shot and now he's got lung fever. The doctor says he needs calomel. Have you got that?"

Joe ran a hand through his wild blond hair. His forehead was pale, shielded by his hat, while the rest of his face was brown as a Laskar's.

"I may have," he said.

He was in a tender position and I understood this. Medicines and other precious commodities had been confiscated by the Federals when they occupied Richmond. Anything Joe and his father had stashed away would be contraband.

"Who are they, these bushwhackers?" he said. "Why did you and your Pa stick your necks out for them?"

Joe's tone of voice said storm clouds were gathering. I dropped my eyes, not wanting to reveal my heart.

"Like I said, they ride with Anderson. The shot one is from Clay County, a boy about your age." I hoped this might inspire in Joe a sense of kinship. "He got hurt a week ago, on the 13th, after that trouble on the Wakenda. The other two are helping us take care of him. Well, they're supposed to be. They're not much use."

"Hattie, are you telling me three of Bill Anderson's men are holed up at your farm?" Joe shook his head with amazement. "Do you know what would happen if the Yankees find out? Your Pa should not have allowed it."

I raised my eyes to Joe's and put some pleading in them. I had to get that calomel for Jesse and if it meant using Joe I'd do it. While I didn't feel good about it, Joe Craighead wouldn't be the first good man to receive treatment he did not deserve.

"Please help, Joe," I said. "He's bad off. And me and Pa, we promised we'd do our best for him. He may be a bushwhacker, but he's Southern like us. Why, things could go hard for us if he dies. Anderson might think we let him go on purpose."

A customer entered the store. We heard Harley greet him, followed by laughter. Joe went to the curtain and peered out. He was thinking, weighing each argument in the balance, I saw it in his eyes. Then he looked at me and without a word walked to the desk, dropped to his knees, and reached his hand up into a secret hidey hole. He pulled out a canvas bag.

"What is it you need?" Joe said. "Calomel?"

I nodded.

Joe fished through the bag and pulled out a small bottle. He gave it to me.

"It's a mixture of mercury and quinine," he said. "Union doctors value it highly so it's in short supply. Be careful with it."

He put the bag back in its hole and got to his feet.

"How will you carry it?" he said. "You're likely to be stopped."

I smiled and untied the strings of my bonnet; I'd already thought of that. That morning I paid special attention to my hair, braiding it in coils on either side of my head—a fashion I disliked ordinarily—then wrapping rolls of black velvet around the coils as I had seen done in *Godey's*. With Joe looking on, I carefully removed the velvet from one coil, slipped the calomel vial inside the braid, repinned the velvet, replaced my straw bonnet, and tied the sash in a bow under my chin.

"There," I said with a bright smile. "You see? The Yankees won't find it there!"

I was feeling well pleased with myself and anxious to get started for home, yet Joe's long face gave me pause.

"Why does this boy mean so much to you, Hattie?" he said. "Is there something between you two?"

"No, Joe, nothing at all. Like I said, me and Pa, we're just trying to do right by him. It's what we'd want done if it was Doak hurt somewhere."

Joe looked unconvinced so I reached out for his big brown hand and held it between my gloved ones.

"It's what I'd want done if it was you, Joe. I'd do all this and more, if it was you."

He smiled then and I saw some relief in it. My heart twisted a bit.

I walked out onto the boardwalk and Joe followed me after a short talk with Harley. Despite the overcast, the sky was bright in comparison with the darkness of the store. Cy, Earl Smith, and Kitt watched me with anxious eyes as I approached the wagon. Earl got up on his bandy hind legs with his paws on the side rail, and Cy's mule tied to the ringbolt let out a honk. They were ready to get under way.

Joe put his hands on my waist and lifted me up on the bench like I was no heavier than a sack of potatoes. Harley came from the store packing a box. He could hardly manage it, what with his crutches, so Joe quick took the box from him and set it in the back of the wagon.

"You can't head home from town without groceries," he said, tying down a canvas cover to protect the contents. "Wouldn't look right."

He was right; I hadn't thought of that in my hurry to get back to Jesse.

"Thank you, Joe," I said. "We'll pay you for all this when Pa sells his crop."

He waved his hand.

"I don't care about that, Hattie." His eyes held mine for longer than was comfortable. "You know I don't."

Cy took up the reins and got Kitt moving. We rode in silence until we were out of town. Only then did I remember Pa's letter still in my waist pocket. I forgot to post it. I took it out, opened the envelope, and started to read. While this was not a noble thing to do, I was curious and of a rebellious frame of mind. Anyhow, I would reseal it and mail it next trip to town.

August 20, 1864
Dear Son,
    It has been a while since your sister and me heard from you. Hattie goes to town every Tuesday and comes back with the dry goods but no letter. She don't say it but she is worried and so am I. Please write and give us some ease.
    Things are not good here Doak and I will not say otherwise. Me and Cy will not have much crop this year. Even if we did I could not get my tobacco to St. Louis because the river is shut down. Yes, it is shut down! Bushwhackers fire on the steamers from the levees at Rocheport and other places and the lily-livered pilots dare not chance it. To a man they are a hifalutin lot of nancy boys and haven't I always said so! The captain of the James White is offering a thousand dollars to any pilot with the balls to steam his boat from St. Louis to Leavenworth and even at that price he can't find one. Anyhow the man from the Camden stemmery was by yesterday and made me an offer and it is not much but I suppose I will take it.
    If this letter falls into Yankee hands I am looking at trouble but I will tell you we have bushwhackers at the house. One of Bill Anderson's boys was chest-shot last week and they brought him here as we are known to be a strong Southern family. I do not know if he will live. Anderson sent two more boys to nurse him and they don't do much of that but they sure eat a lot. Hattie says the two were sent to spy on us, to make sure we don't turn the shot one over to the Feds. In Missouri nobody trusts nobody nowadays.
    Your sister took the fever a while back. She is through it now but she has no meat on her at all and

looks peaked to boot. She hardly talks anymore and fears for you more than is good for her. If your mother was still with us things would be better. Sometimes they were like two cats in a bag, Hattie and your mother, but only because they were so much alike. Hattie will never be a beauty like her mother but she favors her more and more every day. Sometimes when I catch sight of Hattie hanging out the wash, her red hair shining in the sun, well, I can hardly bare to look at her. It is not fair to the child but there it is.

Son, this has not been a cheery letter and I am sorry for it but I will never tell you lies. They say Sterling Price is coming up from Arkansas to liberate Missouri this summer and I hope this is so.

Doak, like I said before I am proud to bursting that a son of mine is soldiering with Old Pap. A finer man never lived and if these bushwhackers around here had any sand they would be with you. If you have a chance tell the general his friend Captain John Rood says hello.

Keep your head down boy and get word to us.
Father

This letter explained some things for me that I guess I would rather not have had explained. My eyes were burning by the end, but I didn't get any sympathy from Cy.

"Serves you right for readin' a letter wasn't meant for you," he said. I reckoned he was right and did not defend myself. We went in silence after that till Earl Smith started cutting up, growling and running in the wagon. Soon enough we saw why: the Yankees we passed on our way into Richmond had set up a roadblock. The snaky officer who eyed me earlier stepped forward and raised his hand to stop us.

"You hold your tongue—hear?" Cy said to me. "None of your sass."

I nodded.

Cy reined in and the Yankee officer took Kitt's bridle.

"Afternoon," he said, smiling and doffing his hat to me like a gentleman which clearly he was not. His teeth were yellow and his face was puffy, with an unhealthy sheen to it. Kitt didn't cotton to him either; she tossed her head and tried to pull away but he held on all the tighter.

"What's your business today, miss?" he said to me. "What brings you out on this hot August afternoon?"

Cy answered. "Shopping in Richmond."

The officer turned his reptile eyes on Cy.

"I was addressing the young lady," he said.

"Shopping in Richmond," I said.

Earl chose this moment to start barking.

"Quiet that dog or I'll do it for you," the Yankee officer said, touching the pistol at his waist. I shushed Earl Smith who sat down all a-tremble.

"Tom," the officer spoke to a soldier behind him without taking his eyes off me. "Take a look in that box."

A few fat drops of rain fell as the soldier walked round to the rear of the wagon, untied the canvas, and peered in. I held my breath for fear the Yankee would ask what we bought. I had no idea what Joe had given us.

"Just stuff," the soldier said, rifling through the contents. "Lard, candles, a bolt of cloth. Housekeeping stuff." He was a tall, handsome man with red hair and freckles who appeared not to relish his work. He retied the canvas cover carefully.

"Don't want your things getting wet." He gave me a friendly smile.

The heavy drops were falling faster, exploding in the dirt like tiny bombs.

"Can we go now?" I said.

The officer cocked his head and regarded me with half-closed eyes.

"What's your hurry?" he said. "Why don't you just climb on down from there for a minute?"

The blood whooshed in my ears so loud I could hardly

hear my own voice.

"What for?" I said.

"Because I said so."

I felt Cy tense up beside me.

"What's this about?" he said. "You got no call to hold us."

The officer unholstered his pistol and pointed it at Cy's face.

"You want to lose the other eye, old man?"

I touched Cy on the arm and stepped down from the wagon. The rain was coming down hard and my dress was soaked through and sticking to my body. My hat was wet, too, and I worried about my cargo.

"That's a pretty dress you've got on." The officer's snake eyes ran me up and down. "Nice and full through the skirt. I like those skirts you Southern girls wear. I bet you girls hide lots of pretty things under those skirts."

"Captain Cheney," the soldier, Tom, said. "Leave her be."

Tom's worried face frightened me. He knew what kind of man this Yankee was, what he was capable of.

"We are for the Union," I said. "I am not a Southern girl. What makes you say it?"

The officer's sly eyes narrowed.

"I can tell," he said. "I can always tell. Tom, come hold this horse. And girl, you come on over here with me." He gestured with a gauntleted hand toward a stand of brush beside the road. "We're going to have us a look-see at what you've got under those skirts. I'll bet it's real sweet."

Cy stood in the wagon, still holding Kitt's reins.

"Lay a hand on her and I'll kill you, you Yankee bastard!" he said.

The officer turned and, quick as a hiccup, shot Cy full in the face. The bullet went in just below his dead eye and out the top of his head in a rosy pink spray that sent his hat spinning high through the air like a whirligig. Till the day I die I will not forget the surprise on Cy's face as he fell to the ground. There he lay still as a sack of grain, mouth open, his good eye fixed heavenward.

"Now come here," the Yankee said, waving his pistol at me. "And be quick about it!"

I stood stricken, unable to move. Earl Smith was barking again—I scarcely heard him above the rain and my own pounding heartbeats—but I saw the officer turn his murderous hand in Earl's direction. His doggy luck held; before the Yankee could pull the trigger the woods came alive with rebel-yelling bushwhackers, flying out of the timber on thundering horses, pistols blazing fire. The first to fall was the soldier Tom who took a bullet in the back, squarely between the shoulder blades.

I took cover behind poor Cy's mule, squatting in terror at the rear of the wagon as the bullets zipped by like deadly insects. One of the bushwhackers rode down on me and before I had time to decide whether to run or fight he lifted me from my feet with one long arm around my waist and swung me up in the saddle behind him. A kerchief covered his face from the eyes down, yet I knew him right off.

"Hold on, Hattie!" Frank said. "Hold tight as you can!"

"Frank! Oh, Frank! Did you see poor Cy? Did you see what they did to him?"

"I saw."

We raced headlong into the woods, jumping fallen trees and fording a steep ravine till we reached a place he judged safe. I slid to the ground.

"Did you get Jesse's medicine?" he said.

I put my hand to my head. My hat was sideways but underneath the velvet roll was in place.

"I have it," I said. "But Cy! Poor Cy! They killed him!"

I was crying hard and my nose ran. Frank took off his handkerchief and gave it to me.

"We'll take care of that Yankee, Hattie, don't you worry about that. Meantime, you stay right here till I get back."

He spurred his horse toward the sound of the action, leaving me alone with nothing but the hickory trees and the squirrels for company. Cy's death played over and over in my head, the surprise on his face, the way his hat sailed through the air like it was tossed at a wedding. I pondered the cheapness of human life, how one man can end another without one ounce of feeling, without regret. Death itself was not new to me; I had seen it before, hard death too, like Ma and cousin Sky, but still the true frailty of the human vessel was unknown to me until now.

From my place of hiding I could hear the sounds of the fight, gunfire and the screams of men and animals. The rain had stopped and when the wind was right I caught the smell of gunpowder. The shots were beginning to taper off when something or someone came crashing through the woods in my direction.

"Frank?" I called. "Is that you?"

There was no answer. I picked up my skirts and started to run when Earl Smith trotted out of the brush. My knees went soft and rubbery with relief. I picked him up and kissed his familiar brown face. Together thus we sat and waited.

Gradually the shooting stopped except for the occasional single report, the terminus, I supposed, of a wounded man or animal. The quiet that followed was worse than the fighting. Who had won? The bushwhackers or the Federals? Despite Frank's admonition, my curiosity got the better of me and I crept through the brush, carrying Earl, till I reached the edge of the wood.

There, on his knees in the muddy road and begging for his life, was the Yankee officer who shot Cy. Two bushwhackers stood before him; one was tall and thin with long, dark hair that hung in curls to his shoulders. The other was short and pale with a freckled face and cheery smile. This short one held a pistol.

"What shall we do with him, Captain?" he said to his long-haired companion.

"Why, parole him of course," said the other.

The Yankee's face lit up with surprised relief just before

the small man raised his pistol and sent a bullet into his brain. Numb with horror I watched as the shooter straddled the Yankee's chest and lopped off his ears. He giggled as he cut and it was a strange, girlish sound.

I stepped out onto the road, looking for Cy, and found him where he fell, his head turned to an unnatural angle. His mule, still tied to the wagon, leaked blood from a bullet hole on his right haunch. Poor Pa, I'd cost him Cy and maybe a mule too.

"Hattie! I told you to stay where I left you!"

Frank walked toward me with a scowl, leading his horse. He was accompanied by a stocky fellow with sloping shoulders and a broad, fleshy face. Behind them bushwhackers bent to their unholy business, scalping Yankees and taking ears like a tribe of red Indians. Even though the dead men were our enemies, this nasty business sickened me.

"Don't scold her now, Franklin," the stocky man said. "The young lady has been through a bad time. She doesn't need to be fussed at, she needs to get home. Am I right?"

I was cold and wet and wanted to get home very much indeed. When Frank's friend offered to drive me, I looked to Frank for reassurance.

"You can trust him, Hattie. He's a friend. Go with him now and get that medicine to Jesse. I'll be along directly."

Within minutes Cy's broken body was under a Union blanket in the back of the buckboard and we were under way. The wounded mule followed along behind, limping piteously. The bushwhackers helped themselves to Joe's groceries and I didn't try to stop them. I didn't care.

"Too bad about the old man," the stranger said. "Was he kin to you?"

"Not kin but good as."

This fellow seemed nice enough but I was not in a mood for talking. My head was full of the things I'd seen and worry for how I would find Jesse, also for how Pa would take Cy's death. My companion, though, was gregarious and inclined to conversation.

"You're lucky we came along when we did," he said. "That Yankee would have done you harm."

"I know it. Thank you, Mr..."

"Coleman Younger. My friends call me Cole. May I call you Hattie?"

"Thank you, Cole, for depriving him of the opportunity."

I sensed a thick streak of the Philadelphia lawyer in this Cole Younger.

He commenced then to tell me his personal story, which was a hard one. Before the war his father was mayor of Harrisonville and the family had a fine house there and big farms in Cass and Jackson counties. Then, a sad event that was all too common, the militia gunned down the father and left him to die in the road. After, they went to Cole's mother's farm and forced her to put the torch to her own house in the dead of winter and her with four little ones yet at home. As if this weren't bad enough, one of Cole's cousins was among those killed when the Federal women's prison collapsed in Kansas City. Her crushed body was pulled from the ruins along with the remains of Josephine Anderson, sister to bushwhacker chieftain Bill Anderson. Another of Bloody Bill's sisters was horribly maimed.

"Although Bill's methods are coarse," Cole said, "he and I do share a bond and I understand his need for reprisal. What the Yankees did to our women was done in cold blood. Vengeance is necessary."

The rain stayed away the rest of the afternoon and the sun did too. That seemed fitting enough to me as sunshine would have been out of place on such a day. It was near dark when at last we turned off the river pike and onto the narrow road that led to our house. I was relieved to see a light in the loft window.

Cole saw the light too.

"So how is brother Dingus?" he said.

"He's in a bad way," I said. "I'm doing all I can for him."

I did not say I was sick with dread, that if I found Jesse dead in the loft I would be grieved beyond measure, beyond all toleration, but crafty Cole sensed it.

"I take it you are sweet on him," he said. "Are you sweet on Franklin's younger brother?"

He applied the crop to Kitt's backside.

"I don't see how that concerns you."

He shrugged his sloping shoulders.

"I don't mean to offend, Hattie," he said. "You seem like a nice young lady. In fact, you remind me of one of my own sisters. I wouldn't want to see you hurt. That's all."

"Why would Jesse hurt me? Why do you say that?" I said. "Has Jesse given you cause to dislike him?"

"It's not about liking. Jesse is a likable fellow and good company. But I'm not sure I trust him, not like I do Frank."

Part of me wanted to hear more but another, bigger part of me didn't. The matter was settled for me anyhow because just then Pa appeared at the barn door carrying a lantern. I told Cole to stop the wagon and jumped down.

"Thank you for driving me home," I said. "Tell Pa what happened and explain about Cy."

With that I ran toward the house without stopping even though Pa called my name. I took the stairs two at a time and flew up the ladder into the loft. Jess was alive; his rattling breath was music to my ears.

"Jesse." I dropped to my knees by the cot. "Jesse. I'm back."

"Hattie?" He opened his eyes. "Water. I need water."

"I've got your medicine," I said. "You're going to be all right."

I took up the pitcher by his bed and found it empty. How long had he been thirsting like this? What was wrong with Pa and those good-for-nothings Nat Tigue and Ol Shepherd? I would give them what for!

"What happened to you?" he said. "Are you all right?"

I had forgotten my muddy dress and generally mussed-up condition. I untied my bonnet and pulled it off.

"We met with some trouble but never you mind. I'll tell you later."

But he insisted on knowing so I told him, leaving out the parts about the Yankee officer's behavior toward me and Cy's murder. Because I thought he might not like it, I also did not tell him about Cole Younger driving me home. As I talked I unpinned the velvet roll from my hair and freed the glass vial. My braid came unbound in the process.

"Do the other one," he said.

I did not understand what he meant.

"Your hair. Let down the other side."

I did as he asked, releasing my hair and letting it hang to my shoulders.

"You should always wear it down like that," he said with frank admiration. "It suits you."

My heart beat fast and faster. Our eyes met and much was said between us without any spoken words. But then, unwelcome and unbidden, Cole Younger's warning came back to me bringing a flicking snake tongue of doubt. Maybe I should resist my emotion, maybe I should not trust this blue-eyed boy who might be a rounder and could die anyhow.

"Save your strength, Jesse James," I said. "You're going to need it."

Chapter Twelve

The next days are a golden blur in my memory, a time of trial, fear, and hardship but also great reward. I stayed by Jesse's bedside for three days and nights running, suffering with him in that cookbox of an attic by day, rejoicing in the cooling river breezes that visited us at night. I grew skilled at all aspects of nursing, so quick and efficient that I fancied myself a rival to Mother Bickerdyke herself. I administered medicine on time, never missing a single dosing; I became adept at changing a man's bed with the man still in it; I discovered that a cloth soaked in water and camphor cooled fevered flesh better than water alone.

Another thing I learned was how to bathe a man in full using a basin and rag. Jesse was at his weakest when I did this, cleansing the long, muscular length of his arms and legs with a warm, soapy cloth. I did not touch him in any wanton or unchristian manner, but even so, despite his profound illness, my ministrations evoked a manly response in him that was most noticeable. Even though I was unschooled in the ways of the marriage bed, any girl with brothers knew what this was about. It did not disgust me as it should have if I were the modest and God-fearing girl I was raised to be; in fact, I admired Jesse's life force more than ever. His was a force too strong for a bullet and lung fever to dampen.

For these three days I forsook all but the most elemental

of household tasks, the cooking and milking, despite Pa's glowering anger, which he displayed at every opportunity. I felt I deserved it, not just because I caused the death of a good man but because Cy's passing meant a doubling of Pa's workload. Still, I saw Fritz Heizinger and other neighbors working in our fields and could be Pa pressed Nat and Ol into service as well; truth is, I do not know how Pa managed during this time, so consumed was I by my attentions to Jesse.

Finally, on the fourth day I woke on my straw pallet beside his cot to see Jesse up on one elbow looking at me in the blue morning light. It was like he'd seen me with my clothes off or something.

"Hello Hattie," he said. "Did you know you look like an angel when you sleep?"

A thrill ran through me. I sat up and touched his cheek. He was cool! His fever had broken!

"You should have woke me up. How long were you watching me?"

"A while." He smiled. "I didn't want to wake you. I liked looking."

I got up and smoothed my dress. I could not look at him.

"Are you hungry? You want breakfast?"

"I am hungry," he said. "I believe I could eat a horse entire."

I fixed him dry toast and broth and he took it well, so at noon I stepped him up to oatmeal with milk and brown sugar. For dinner I prepared an eggy custard with vanilla extract and a generous dollop of cream from the ice box in the cellar. All day I went about my work like I had wings on my feet. Pa noticed this change in my demeanor.

"So, I take it our friend is recovering?" he said, lighting his pipe. "About ready to move on, is he?"

"He is better, Pa, but only just. He's not ready to ride yet."

Pa watched me collect the plates from the table, squinting at me through his pipe smoke. The weight of his eyes made me uncomfortable and I dropped a saucer that broke to bits.

"The Feds are arresting whole families on suspicion of helping the bushwhackers," he said as I picked up pieces of saucer and dumped them in the dust bin. "They're holding them—men, women and little children—in the Warrensburg jail. And that's not even the worst of it. I can't tell you some things I've heard. They're especially keen to catch anyone who rides with Bill Anderson."

I kept my eyes on my work, scraping the leavings from his plate into the slop pail. Pa went on.

"Did I tell you Allen McReynolds is dead?" McReynolds was a boyhood friend of Pa's who lived to the east, in Saline County. "I just heard yesterday. Militia came to his house dressed like bushwhackers, tricked him into feeding them, giving advice about folks who might take them in, safe places to hide, and whatnot. Then they called him out for a traitor and shot him dead, right in front of his wife and children."

I filled the sink with warm water from the kettle on the stove. Pa was building his case like a Philadelphia lawyer.

"The point is, Hattie, we got to get that boy out of here. Him and them others." Anticipating my reply, he raised his pipe hand against my words. "It was me let them in, I know it, and I'm sorry I did. It seemed right at the time but now they got to move on. The Feds already suspect us on account of Ben and Doak and you know it. They find them bushwhackers here and they'll finish us off sure this time. It's too dangerous, Hattie, too dangerous by half. Any day someone might turn us in. A man can't trust nobody these days and that's the sorry truth."

I scooped some soft soap from the dish above the sink and swished my hand through the water, raising a suds. Even if I agreed with him in wanting Jesse gone, which of course I did not, there was one big factor Pa was not considering. Bill Anderson wanted Jesse here till he was well enough to ride and Bloody Bill was the one calling the shots. A man who shakes hands with the devil has a hard time getting his hand back. Wasn't it Pa himself told me that?

"I know it." I would not rile Pa. Best keep him cool. "You are right, Pa. This could be trouble for us. There's a chance of it. But there's another side too. Jesse is strong, he'll be ready soon enough and then Bill Anderson will owe us. That could be a good thing. That might help us get our tobacco to market. Just give Jess a bit longer, Pa. Just a bit."

He studied me with narrowed eyes and for a moment I thought I might've given myself away about reading that letter to Doak when Pa complained about Anderson stopping the river traffic. But that wasn't why he was looking at me funny.

"You best not be losing your head over that boy, Hattie," he said; there was some heat in his voice. "Don't be forgetting you're promised to Joe Craighead, or good as. There's no future for you and that James boy. None a-tall. You hear me, girl?"

"I hear you, Pa."

I turned back to my sink full of dishes, grateful he could not see my face. Poor Pa. I didn't want to hurt him but he was in for some mighty big surprises.

Chapter Thirteen

August gave way to September, and an unusually fine one too, weather-wise, anyhow. The colors came early; the sugar maple in front of our house glowed like an embering fire and the cottonwoods along the river added splashes of persimmon-yellow and pumpkin-orange to the mix. Truly, I couldn't remember a more beautiful autumn, but then it might have had something to do with my felicitous state of mind.

This, despite the fact that the war in Missouri was at its meanest. The rumor was Price and his army would be coming any day now, coming to rid us of our Yankee occupiers. This had everybody whipped up, not only the Yankees but the bushwhackers too, who took it on themselves to keep the Federals busy north of the Missouri River so Old Pap could advance unimpeded. The country was in a fever; every day brought reports of terrible depredations, mostly by Bill Anderson—or W. Anderson, commander of the Kansas First Guerillas, as he had been calling himself in his frequent letters to the Lexington newspapers. In addition to the scalpings and ear-takings, there was whispered talk of beheadings, skinned bodies hanging in trees, of salacious attacks on women, black and white.

But terrible though these things were, they did not touch me. I was lifted above the horror by my love for Jesse; it was a guidon flying bold in the wind, a church bell ringing clear and true. Nothing diminished my happiness—not the war, not Pa's sourness, not the maddening presence of mean-eyed Nat and lazy Ol. He didn't have to say it; Jesse felt the same for me. I knew this, despite the suspicions others tried to plant in my heart. Far as Hattie Rood was concerned, things were right with the world.

Every day I rushed through my chores to spend time with him and my attentions produced a healthy result. Each day, more color returned to his face and his eyes grew brighter. I enjoyed housekeeping for him as I did for no one else. I got that dusty old loft looking nice and cozy, scrubbing the floor with sand till it was clean enough to eat on, and sewing curtains from leftover dress fabric that was light blue in color with pale yellow flowers. Jesse objected, proclaiming them girly, but the colors were cheering, and on sunny days the light shining through the cloth lent the room a cooling, underwater aspect. I was proud of them.

By now Jess was able to sit up in bed to take his meals and it occurred to me that his returning strength would open our romance to whole new possibilities! We would walk out together, down to the river maybe, and when he was strong enough to ride I would take him to a place me and Doak found a couple years back, a cave in one of the limestone bluffs along the river with an ancient skeleton inside and weird drawings on the walls.

Like I said, nothing dimmed my happiness, and this was true with the exception of Pa and Joe Craighead. Joe especially was a pain in my heart and an ache in my soul. The Sunday after we buried Cy in the family plot under the oak in the back field, Joe came to take me riding. I forgot he was coming, even though he reminded me at the funeral. Joe showed up in his buggy while I was out back hanging wash on the line. In particular I was hanging Jesse's border shirt which I'd mended and scrubbed the blood stains out of. When Joe rounded the corner of the house and saw me so occupied, the corners of his mouth went down in a way I'd seen a thousand times since we were children. Joe Craighead never was one could hide his feelings.

"Those bushwhackers still here then?" he said.

I said hello Joe and turned back to my laundry. I wasn't one to hide my feelings either and I did not want to see Joe right now.

"Didn't that medicine take?"

"It took."

"Then why's he still here? And why aren't you dressed to go riding?"

I took up Jesse's underdrawers and pinned them on the line.

"Don't' do that!" Joe said, scandalized. "Don't be handling his skivvies like that. It's not proper!"

I laughed at that—I couldn't help it. Proper! There was no such thing nowadays! Proper went out the door when War came in, and I reckon Proper tipped his hat in passing! Who did Joe think had been nursing Jesse all this time, keeping him clean, emptying his night pot, tending to his human needs? Nat and Ol?

"What's so funny?" Joe said.

"Hellfire, Joe! It's just underwear! I never knew you were such a maiden lady!"

That hurt him. I wished I hadn't said it.

"I ain't that," he said. "It's only I don't relish coming to take you riding and finding the woman I aim to marry washing another man's laundry. I'm just saying."

That was the first time he had ever said the word "marry" straight out. I pinned Pa's nightshirt on the line. The silence between me and Joe was heavy as iron.

"Well?" he said. "Don't you got nothin' to say?"

I made myself look at him. He was holding his hat, turning it in his hands; his hair was parted and wet-combed to the side. He must've used some sort of pomade or macassar to make it lie flat. I took a big breath and steeled my heart for what I had to do.

"I don't want to get married Joe, not to you, not to anybody. It's not that I don't care for you—I do, you know it—I just don't want to be a wife yet. Not yours, not anybody's. I am not ready."

He looked at his feet and I saw he was wearing new boots, shiny black and stiff-looking. Those boots and the slicked-down hair nearly broke my heart.

"I bet you'd say different if Jesse James asked you," he said.

A jolt of lightning shot through me. How did he know Jesse's name?

"That's right—I know who your bushwhacker is!" Joe was getting red in the face. "I know he's from Centerville in Clay County and a lot of other things too! Like how his Pa run off to California and left his family high and dry on account of the mother is a hellion—the worst woman in Missouri I hear! How she's been three times married and leads that simple fellow she's with now round like a steer with a ring through his ear! Bet he didn't tell you about none of that, did he?"

He did not, but it wouldn't matter to me if Jesse's people were kin to Black Abe himself.

"Joe..."

He interrupted.

"Them Jameses, him and his brother, they are border trash! The brother was with Quantrill at Lawrence and maybe Jesse was too. Who knows? He's no good, that Jesse James, he won't treat you right, Hattie. Not like I would."

My kindly feelings toward Joe were dissolving fast.

"And you know all this how, Joe Craighead?" I tried to stay calm but my steam was building. "Have you been going around asking questions? I surely do hope not because that's dangerous for me and Pa. You could bring the Yankees right down on top of us! And another thing—just 'cause we've known each other all this time does not mean you own me! You don't know everything about me. You might think you do but you don't! Besides, Jesse would never hurt me. He owes me his life—he says so."

Joe gave a short laugh and shook his head.

"Hattie, you don't know how boys are. He'll say whatever you want to hear. That's how they do, his kind." He pressed his lips together and shook his head again. "I wish Doak was here. He'd see it right; he'd make you see the truth."

"Oh well," I said, defiant, "he isn't. And even if he was, it wouldn't change nothing. Doak doesn't do my thinking for me. Nobody thinks for me but me. Hattie Rood."

We eyed each other for a time, then Joe sighed and stuck his hat on so hard the brim pushed out the tops of his ears. It was comical-looking but I didn't feel like laughing.

"All right, Hattie," he said. "Have it your way. If you change your mind, I'll wait—for a while anyhow."

He walked back to his buggy, his shoulders sagging; all my anger at him melted away. I felt awful seeing him sad like that and knowing I was the cause of it. We went far back together, me and Joe, and despite what I said about him not knowing all there was about me, he pretty much did. In fact, he knew me better than anyone and he liked me anyhow. That was saying something. Part of me wanted to run after him and tell him we could be together like he wanted. That would be the safe thing; Joe was reliable and kind and he loved me. It would make Pa happy too, and not just because of the Craigheads' money. But I didn't run after him. Instead I finished hanging the wash and watched him drive off in his buggy.

That night, a sweet September evening with a full moon and cool river breeze, Frank came to the house. He was unshaven and his clothes smelled of horse sweat and wood smoke. I hadn't seen him for a week, not since the trouble on the Richmond pike, and I wanted to hear what was going on in the bush. But it was clear I wasn't wanted up in the loft when men were talking business, so I listened from my bedroom, sitting cross-legged on the floor. I heard Frank tell

Jesse how their good friend Fletch Taylor had quit the war. Seemed he had barely recovered from the amputation of his right arm when one of his fellow bushwhackers accidentally shot him in the other.

"Is he going to lose that one too?" Jess asked. "Will Fletch have no arms a-tall?"

"No, but he's done just the same," Frank said. "He wants it spread around he's dead so the Yankees won't look for him."

"Yankees!" I recognized Nat's nasal voice. "Fletch Taylor has more to fear from Bill Quantrill than any damn Yankees! Them two been out for each other since that business in Texas last winter. Quantrill shouldn't never have tried to get Fletch arrested."

"Fletch killed a officer," Ol said. "A Confederate officer."

"No matter," said Nat. "He was one of us, Fletch. Quantrill was wrong to turn on him." This met with murmurs of agreement.

"I can't hardly believe it," Jesse said. "Fletch was the last one I figured to lose his purpose."

Frank had more bad news. Another friend, Dick Yager, had been shot in the head while fighting in Arrow Rock. He didn't die right off; his fellow bushwhackers took him to the house of a Southern supporter, just like Jesse was brought to us, but someone ratted Yager out to the Feds. They sent a death patrol to finish him off.

"Damn!" Again, Nat's voice. "Dick owed me money! I wonder if his brother is good for it."

"You'll never see that money, Tigue," Frank said. "'He that dies pays all debts.' "

"Says who? That limey Shakespeare you're always gassing on about?"

I was curious to know what happened to the family who sheltered the unfortunate Yager, but that part of the story did not interest the others. Since Yager's death, Frank said, Dave Pool, George Todd, and their boys were laying low, riding out every now and then to rob a stage, cut a telegraph line, or terrorize the Missouri Pacific workers laying rail from Warrensburg to Kansas City.

"So Anderson's got the show all to himself now," Frank said. "There's a hundred men with him at Rocheport. You should see it, brother. It looks like a regular army camp and a Federal camp at that, since most of the boys wear blue uniforms. He asks about you, Jesse, Bill does, says you have potential. Wants to know how you're getting on, if the Roods are taking good care of you. He wants you back, and soon. Camp is only two easy days' ride from here. Way you look now, it shouldn't be long."

I held my breath. Jesse's response would say a lot about his feelings for me and his plans for our future. He did not want to leave me, I knew he didn't! Anyhow, he wasn't ready to ride again, not by a long shot. Why, he wasn't even on his feet yet, he hadn't even come downstairs to take a meal at the table. There were so many things me and him hadn't done. I was thinking so hard about these things I missed Jesse's answer, if he spoke one.

That night I slept in Doak's room. Sleep was hard to catch, though, and I was still awake when Nat and Ol climbed from the loft, and later still when Frank did the same sometime after midnight.

What would I do if Jesse left? How could I bear it?

Chapter Fourteen

The next day Jesse surprised me by coming downstairs at noon for dinner. It was the first time I'd seen him on his feet and I was surprised how tall he was, nigh to six feet or thereabouts. I was in the kitchen frying up a string of catfish Ol caught that morning. The lazy fellow finally found a use for his worthless self. When it came to cooking I was nowhere near the pride of Ray County, although I did know how to fry catfish, having watched Jerusha do it often enough when I was coming up. The key was in knowing just the right mix of cornmeal, flour, and salt to use in the dredge, and you had to use thick, sweet buttermilk instead of plain to make the dredge stick right. Also, you needed a shallow skillet—a spider worked best—fired to just the right heat when you dropped the fish in or it would come out soggy. Finally, it was best if you had olive oil for the fry. This I had, thanks to Joe. Fixed this way it was pretty near impossible to beat fresh Missouri River catfish for good eating.

I guess it was the smell brought Jesse to my kitchen. He was pale, like the climb down the ladder and stairs was a hard one. With his shirt on and all the way buttoned, and his long hair combed back from his face, he looked older, less a boy and more a man. I felt a stirring inside me.

He grinned and took a seat at the table.

"That fish almost ready?" He tucked a napkin into his

collar. "Sure smells good."

Thrilled as I was to see him up and about, I was a touch worried, too. Why was he pushing himself all of a sudden? Was it so he could join Anderson's camp in Rocheport?

I forked a golden piece of catfish and put it on newspaper to drain.

"Hold onto your patience," I said. "You'll get your share." Along with the fish, I had yeast rolls in the oven, greens and stewed tomatoes from the summer garden, iced milk to drink, and apple cobbler with cream for dessert. I guess I was showing off my kitchen skills some.

I went out back to sound the dinner bell. Naturally Nat and Ol came right in—they never strayed far from the house at meal time—but Pa was nowhere to be seen.

Again I rang. The bell usually brought Earl Smith running but I didn't see him either. I called but nothing happened. Behind me I heard Nat and Ol sitting down at the table, filling their plates. I scanned the fields of ripening tobacco, the oily leaves green and yellow in the bright September sun, then the barn and smokehouse; still no sign of Pa. I went inside to set aside his dinner. If I didn't, everything would be gone by the time he showed up.

Nat and Ol kept stuffing their faces, but I felt Jesse's eyes on me the whole time.

"Where's your Pa?" he said.

This got Nat's attention. He raised his head, fixing his beady black eyes on me as he chewed.

"I don't know," I said. "I'm putting food back for him, then I'll go look."'

Jesse set down his fork and got to his feet.

"No." His voice was different, harder than usual. "You stay here. Nat and Ol will go."

The two bushwhackers didn't appear too happy about this, especially Nat.

"Maybe when I'm done. I ain't done yet."

"Yes, you are," Jesse said in his new voice. "Go find

Captain Rood. Might be something's wrong."

For the first time I sensed Jesse held some privileged place in this bushwhacker world, something I had not perceived before because of his illness. Nat gave him the evil eye but did not argue. Ol rose from the table with one yeast roll in his mouth and another in his shirt pocket for later. They were at the kitchen door when Jesse stopped them.

"Quiet!" He raised his hand and we stood like statues. Earl was carrying on out front of the house. Jesse turned to me.

"Hattie, see who it is. If it's Feds or that boyfriend of yours, get rid of them. We'll be watching from the front room." He touched his side and only then did I notice the pistol tucked into his belt.

This new Jesse was someone I did not know. The shining blue eyes were those of a stranger.

I did like he said. My shoes sounded unusually loud on the floorboards as I walked through the house and stepped out on the porch. Behind me I heard Jesse, Nat, and Ol taking positions at the parlor windows.

The midday sun was hot. A droplet of sweat ran between my breasts as I waited. Had someone ratted us out? Was Pa swinging from a tree somewhere? Or maybe being tortured by bluebellies asking about Anderson and his guerillas? And me, was I about to find myself in the middle of a gunfight between Federal troops and the bushwhackers in my mother's parlor?

As if reading my thoughts, Jesse spoke from the window behind me.

"It's all right, Hattie. I won't let anything happen to you. I promise."

Earl's barking was getting louder and I told myself this was a good sign. If our visitors were Jayhawkers or Federals they would have shot him or cut his throat by now. Finally two men, walking side by side, appeared on the river road with Earl Smith trotting at their feet. My heart jumped up in my throat. One of the men was Pa, I recognized his stooped, lanky frame. The other was taller and rail thin, and he moved slowly, leaning on a crutch. Pa carried the stranger's bedroll and knapsack.

Before I knew it I was running top speed down the drive toward them, holding my skirt up above my knees so it wouldn't slow me down, and straight into my brother's open arms.

Chapter Fifteen

Doak dropped his crutch and hugged me tight, lifting me off the ground. I was surprised at the strength in him because he was awful thin. I felt sharp bones under his baggy brown coat. I kissed him on the cheek, tasting road dust and salt. I hadn't fully realized how much I missed him till now.

After a time he set me down and held me at arm's length, keeping his hands on my shoulders.

"Stand back, Hat," he said. "Let's get a proper look at you."

I dropped a curtsy, like I was at a cotillion. He shook his head and made a heavy show of disappointment.

"Oh well," he said, "I suppose there must be some fellow somewhere who'll settle for a skinny, red-headed gal. But he better come along soon, right Pa? 'Fore she gets even worse?"

I made a face at him. Back in the old days I would have given him some of his own, saying he wasn't such a prize himself, but I didn't. Doak looked tired and old and not much like the nineteen-year-old boy who left here all those months ago. I picked up his crutch and gave it to him. Then the four of us—me, Doak, Pa, and Earl—started back to the house. As we walked I saw the curtains stirring. I wondered if Pa had told Doak about our visitors. I sensed he hadn't and I didn't say anything either. Doak wouldn't like it and I wanted to prolong the joy of his homecoming long as possible.

"What happened to your leg?" I said.

"I hurt it in a fight with a company of Yankees. Saved my entire regiment. Why, I'm surprised you didn't read about it in the papers."

I rolled my eyes. "What happened to your leg?" I said.

"I fell off my horse." He smiled at me and I saw—despite his thinness—he still had his dimples. Girls loved Doak's dimples.

"*You* fell off a horse?" I couldn't believe it. Doak rode like a Tartar.

"Yes, I did. Truth is, I was drunk at the time. Stiff as a mitten."

I shot a look at Pa to see how he would receive this shocking admission. Someone in the family may have had a weakness at one time—such things were not discussed with me—but now drunkenness was a thing not tolerated in the Rood household. Pa very rarely broke temperance and only on special occasions. But on this occasion he said nothing, just kept his eyes on the ground and kept walking. I understood then—Doak was a grown man in Pa's eyes, no longer a child to be chastened and scolded.

When we were almost to the house Nat stepped out onto the porch, scratching himself with one hand and holding his revolver in the other. He favored us with one of his yellow smiles.

"Hello, Captain Rood," he said. "We was wondering where you was at. Who's this you got with you?"

Doak stopped short. "Pa?"

Pa made no attempt to hide his dislike.

"Doak, this is Nat Tigue. He's a bushwhacker and there's two more like him inside. They been staying with us on account of one was shot and they're hiding out here till he's ready to ride again. I wrote you about them. Didn't you get my letter?"

The letter! I had forgotten all about it! It was still in my underthings drawer!

"No," Doak said. "I got no letter. So, Tigue, who do you ride with?"

Nat puffed his narrow pigeon chest.

"Bill Anderson," he said. "We ride with Bloody Bill hisself."

Doak cussed. Blaspheming was another thing Pa took a dim view of.

"Jesus, Pa! How long they been here?"

"Couple, three weeks."

"Hellfire! What are you thinking, Pa? Do you want to end up like John McFaddin?"

Early in the war our friend and neighbor was gutted like a fish because the militia suspected him of aiding Southern guerillas. The Yankees killed him while his girls begged for his life. The younger daughter, Hannah McFaddin, was Doak's sweetheart at the time. It was partly her father's murder decided him to enlist.

Before Pa could answer, the front door opened and Jesse and Ol joined Nat on the porch. They wore their guns tucked in their belts. When Nat saw this he put his away too.

"You must be the brother Hattie talks about all the time," Jesse said, sitting on a step. "She thinks mighty high of you."

Doak regarded him like he would a riverboat huckster or traveling quacksalver.

"How'd you get that hitch in your step?" Jesse said. "Yankees do it?"

Doak did not try to make himself the hero.

"I had an accident."

"What kind of accident?"

"I fell off my horse."

Jesse grinned.

"Is that so? Well, takes a man to admit it."

Doak did not return Jesse's smile.

"You may as well know I got no use for bushwhackers," he said. "You make things worse for regular folks, like Hattie and Pa. Bill Anderson is the worst of a bad lot. He is a killer and thief of the first water."

Jesse's blue eyes went a shade darker.

"You say that now, but you regulars will see things different soon enough," he said. "You fight with Price, right? Well, Sterling Price needs us. He'll need Anderson and Quantrill and Todd and all us partisan rangers when the liberation starts. We will not disappoint. You'll see."

Doak and Jesse eyed each other like they were about to fight or run a foot race. It occurred to me then, looking at them, that they were a lot alike in many ways. In normal times they would be tight as brothers, but now, times being abnormal, they were just as like to go the other way. I took Doak's arm and steered him for the door.

"Come on to the kitchen," I said. "I'll give you dinner."

Pa followed us inside while Jess and the others stayed out on the porch. I guess they figured we were entitled to some private family time. Doak put his upset aside long enough to go at his food like a man who hadn't eaten for a week, and skinny as he was I reckon he hadn't. While he ate he answered our questions about soldiering with Old Pap's army, about the retreat deep into Arkansas after the defeat at Pea Ridge, about the long miserable steamboat ride down into Tennessee and then even farther south down into Mississippi and Louisiana. He got angry when he talked about the disrespect Jeff Davis showed Price and his Missourians. The Confederate president pooh-poohed Price's contention that retaking Missouri was key to Southern victory.

"It's finally going to happen, though," Doak said when at last he was done eating. He leaned back in his chair and wiped his mouth with the back of his hand. "Only last month Price got the go-ahead. He was getting his army together when I broke my leg but I figure he'll be crossing into Missouri this month, all goes according to Hoyle."

Pa and I looked at each other. For two years we had been hearing Price was on his way. We'd been hearing it so long it was hard to believe now, even if it was Doak saying it. And even if it was true, well, maybe it was too late.

Doak sensed our skepticism.

"It's true. He'll take St. Louis first."

At this Pa let out a hoot that was the closest to a laugh I'd heard from him in weeks.

"St. Louis! He better have thirty thousand men and four regiments of artillery if he aims to take St. Louis!"

"He has twelve thousand men," Doak said, "and hardly any artillery. He won't need it because what he does have is General Jo Shelby and three divisions of cavalry."

Pa shook his head.

"Son, it will take more than twelve thousand men and General Jo's cavalry to take St. Louis. And what does Price think the Feds will be doing while he's marching through Missouri? Drinking apple brandy and tipping dominoes?"

Doak was surprised and clearly disappointed by Pa's reaction.

"The Yankees are spread thin, fighting bushwhackers," Doak said. "That's the one thing those boys are good for—keeping Yanks busy. That's why Price is coming now. His staff is in contact with the O.A.K.—we can count on thousands of them to join us and probably thousands more from Iowa and Illinois too!"

My heart dropped to my ankles. Was this the kind of hooey Sterling Price used for his decision-making? The Order of American Knights was a secret, pro-slavery pack of blowhards. Any man can say grand things and make big promises in secret. Just ask a woman.

"Not only that," Doak went on, "but of course the people of Missouri will rally in support of our advancing army. The people of Missouri will rise up to rid their brothers and sisters of the Northern invader!"

I busied myself washing dishes. I didn't look at Pa but I knew his thoughts were same as mine. Did Doak really believe all this fiddlefaddle or was he spouting what he heard others say? And if this was Price's grand plan, then for sure the old man had been away from Missouri too long. Our people were too beat down to rise up in support of anything. It might have been different if Price had come last summer, before Quantrill's men depredated in Kansas and brought all hell down on us. That's when all went to smash. The Lawrence business lost Quantrill and his bushwhackers the support of the pro-South common folk and, because of General Ewing's response, turned the western part of our state into a ghostland of burned houses, crumbling smoke-blackened chimneys, empty roads, and dusty, dried-up fields. Now, too late, Old Price and his army were coming to supposedly free the people of Missouri, and in truth they wouldn't do a thing but bring the wrath of the Republican North down upon us even harder than it was already! Yes, the Southern cause was all gone to pie, not only here but across the country. The papers were full of bleak news and nothing but. Sherman took Atlanta on September 1st, and for me that fact alone spoke truth enough. The war was lost. Way I saw it, the only question left was how many more people would die before the men in charge of such things admitted it?

"You tell it right, friend." Jesse spoke from the kitchen door where he had come on catspaw. "Missouri people will stand with Price, and us guerillas will do our part, and together we'll send the pigs skedaddling! We'll show them what Secesh round here are made of!"

His blue eyes gleamed, like they were lit from inside.

Pa shook his head with disgust.

"Son, put this notion aside! The Yanks are too many, too many. There's five of them for every one of you." He looked at Doak with a naked pleading in his eyes that hurt me so I had to turn away.

"Don't go back to General Price, boy. You know how I admire the man—haven't I said it over and over—but he will not prevail in this. Beyond that, you're injured. No one would think the less of you if you stay. Me and your sister, we need you. We're hardly getting by. You're the only son I got left." Here his voice trembled. "Don't go dying for something that's already done."

Jesse crossed the room and stopped before my father.

"I'm surprised to hear you say that, Captain Rood. If that's how you feel, why'd you take me in? There was risk for you in it. Why do that if you thought it was finished?"

"I been asking myself that same question," Pa said.

There was an uncomfortable scene, with Pa in his chair and Jess standing in front of him. It lasted for a time; I tried to think of something to say but I couldn't.

"You and Hattie been good to me, Captain," Jess said at last, "and I'm grateful for it, but you'd best be careful what you say. This war ain't finished, sir, not by a long shot. Us boys, we won't never quit fighting—even if Robert Lee and Jeff Davis give it up, we will keep on. We won't never lay down and let Black Abe Lincoln plant his iron boot on the necks of our families. And we'll remember who was with us and who wasn't. You best believe that."

Pa looked up at Jesse without rising from his chair.

"What are you saying, young man?" he said.

In that awful moment I sensed Pa feared Jesse, a boy one-third his age.

"I'm saying, you'd best be clear about your allegiance, Captain Rood. You call yourself a Southern man but loyalty without faith is same as no loyalty at all. There's no half-way in this—a man is all for one thing or all the other. And don't be saying it's finished. It won't never be finished till we drive every last Yankee and nigger-loving abolitionist out of Missouri. This is *our* home. It is worth dying for, and the dying ain't nearly done."

Chapter Sixteen

From that day forward, Jesse spent his waking hours working to harden himself. He walked up and down the porch stairs to rebuild his legs, and lifted full buckets of water time and again to strengthen his arms. He was strong and fullmuscled by nature and he came back fast. I saw improvements in him with each passing day. This raised opposing feelings in me. One, I was glad to see him return to himself, and proud, too, for I knew I had some role in it. But at the same time I feared his recovery would take him away. This was small of me, but there it was.

Him and Pa mostly kept away from each other after that scene in the kitchen, while Doak walked a line between the two. Though he did not like the bushwhacker's methods, Doak sensed a kindred spirit in Jesse, and Jesse, I believe, felt likewise. He liked talking to Doak about the people and things he saw down south, and he was particularly interested in anything having to do with General Jo Shelby. Jess was a great admirer of Shelby, leader of The Iron Brigade, cavalryman and raider extraordinary, capturer of steamships and burner of bridges. Doak was with Shelby in Arkansas at the battles of Cane Hill and Prairie Grove, where General Jo's Missourians made a proud name for themselves holding the center against a ferocious Union attack. Four horses were shot out from under Jo Shelby one bitter December day, all sorrels, and after that Doak said the general would ride nothing else.

"What was the worst fighting you saw?" Jesse asked. "I'd like to hear about that."

They sat at the table drinking coffee while I peeled potatoes at the sink. It was getting on toward dinner, and the sinking sun colored the kitchen in a warm orangey light; one of those special Missouri sunsets we take for our natural due, but that newcomers are much impressed with.

"That's easy enough," Doak said. "It was down in Arkansas at Prairie Grove. Not because of the fight—though that was bad enough—but what came after."

He kept his eyes down on his cup as he told it. It happened on December 7, 1862, not long after he joined the fight. Price's army had tussled with Union forces under Blunt at Cane Hill some two weeks before, and while the boys gave them a good fight, Price's men were badly outnumbered. They had to back out.

"I rode with Shelby's rear guard, covering the retreat, and we took a heavy dose of grape and canister all the way. Blunt's troops caught up with us there at Prairie Grove and we dug in. It was cold that day, cold as a witch's tit—sorry, Hattie—but the place itself was real pretty, you know, like a painting, with haystacks all around, an apple orchard, and a church with a fresh coat of white paint. Even at the time, I thought how sweet that place would be in the spring, with the apple trees flowering and such. Anyhow, that night got real bad, so cold it made your teeth hurt, but Blunt kept on shelling us. The wounded men were suffering something awful. The ones that were able crawled over to the haystacks to get warm."

He went quiet at the memory. Jesse didn't say anything and neither did I. We waited for Doak to tell it.

"Well, what happened was the artillery shells set the hay on fire," he said, "and those boys burned. They were mostly Federal boys because the hayricks were closer to their lines, but that didn't make it any easier to listen to. I never heard screaming like that, and I hope never to again, but there wasn't anything we could do for them. But that wasn't even the worst of it. The smell of roasting meat drew hogs from somewhere and they ate those boys, drug them out of the hay, whole or in parts, and ate them right there on the field. We shot at them but they ran off to the woods with pieces of man hanging out of their mouths. I still sick up when I think of it."

My stomach rolled inside me. Tonight's dinner was meant to be special—hash with carrots, potatoes, and the last of the beef I brined last winter using my own recipe of brown sugar, molasses, and salt—but I doubted I would have an appetite.

I did, though, and so did Pa and the boys. After the meal me, Jess, and Doak went out on the porch to read the Lexington newspapers, which we got whenever someone went to town for the mail. There were two papers printed in that town: The *Lexington Weekly Union*, which as you might guess was pro-Northern in outlook, and the *Lexington Caucasian*, which was pro-South. Jesse was the keenest reader of newspapers I ever saw. He couldn't get his fill of them, reading every word from front to back, and the advertisements too. Lately the news was all about Bill Anderson. On September 3rd his 'whackers killed twelve militiamen in Howard County. Six of Anderson's boys also were killed in that fight, and thirty revolvers found on their bodies.

"Reports have it the area of Boone and Howard counties are virtually swarming with bushwhackers, rebel Confederate bands, and outlaws of all nature," Jesse read to us from the *Weekly Union*. Hearing this news made him hungry to get back in the bush, I could tell.

He read another story about how on the 7th Anderson's boys stopped a freight train near Centralia Station and stole four carloads of horses. Jesse's glee turned to outrage when he read that the Federals were threatening to levy a fine of $15,000 on Confederate sympathizers in the area if the horses weren't returned, which of course they would not be. There also were accounts of the robbery of the Warrensburg mail, of pro-Union families forced to refugee their homes in Lafayette County because of marauding bushwhackers, and of a dust-up between guerilla leader Cliff Holtzclaw—one of Anderson's lieutenants—and Union forces in Howard County, resulting in the death of six rebels.

All this brought color to Jesse's face. He'd be leaving us soon and thinking that made me desperate. I had to figure out a way to make him stay.

The very next day something came to me. I learned through Ol that Jesse had marked his seventeenth birthday on the fifth day of September. I resolved to surprise him with a cake, and not just any cake but one of my special Jenny Linds like I bragged about back when he first came. He said I'd have to show him and I would! I would demonstrate my love. Once he saw how resourceful I was, and the trouble I was willing to put myself through just to please him, he would stick around. Trouble was, this was a rich and showboaty confection, and despite all my boasting I had only made it once before, on Doak's last birthday at home. I could do it again, but it would take some doing, as the makings of a Jenny Lind cake were rare as hen's teeth these days. I'd need eggs, butter, sweet cream, apples and, most precious of all, a lemon—not the powdery stuff they sold in stores to make lemonade, but a lemon entire, juice and rind.

Once the notion came to me, that cake became my obsession. All day long I schemed of ways to acquire the ingredients needed for its manufacture. The butter and cream I could manage, assuming poor old Eugenie would cooperate; the apples and the eggs too. The hens weren't laying now but I had a few eggs socked away in a bucket hanging in the well where they kept cool and fresh. The lemon, though, was a different matter. Craighead's store was out of the question. Even if they had one, a lemon would be expensive and I could not in good conscience take any more of Joe's charity. Nor was he likely to offer it, seeing how things were with us.

Then I thought of it: Hi Braddock! Uncle Hi would have

a lemon if anybody did, and he'd give me one, too. He'd been partial to me ever since the Sunday years ago when he caught the Bledsoe brothers throwing a snake at me after church. It didn't bother me much, the Bledsoes were like that and I wasn't afraid of a black snake anyhow, even though it was an unusually big thick one. But Uncle Hi got mighty put out. He ran the Bledsoes off with a switch, then gave me a linty piece of peppermint from his pocket for my trouble.

"Them Bledsoes won't never amount to nothin'," he said with disgust. "If they was my boys I'd whip 'em good. Throwin' snakes at girls shows poor character." Turned out he was right; the three Bledsoe brothers died young for three different reasons, none good.

Anyhow, that night I went to bed happy because I had a plan. Only a few miles of good road lay between our farm and Uncle Hi's place. If I started early I could be back before anyone missed me.

It was still dark when I got out of bed and dressed myself in Ben's old things. His red flannel shirt hung down to my knees and his trousers would suit only if I rolled the legs and tied a rope round my waist. My hair I braided in one long coil and pinned up under a wide-brimmed straw hat. Before heading downstairs I checked my reflection in my bedroom mirror. I didn't look like much of a boy, but at least I didn't look like a girl, neither.

The air was cold for mid-September. I could see my breath as I walked to the barn where Earl and Kitt were surprised to see me, especially dressed like I was. Kitt cocked her ears and Earl sat at my feet looking into my eyes like he expected some sort of explanation. I talked to them in a low voice as I dug Kitt's tack out of the junk stall, telling them how we were going to Uncle Hi's place for a lemon. This seemed to satisfy. I pulled out my woman's saddle and bridle but then, remembering my disguise, put them back. I would ride astride, the way my brothers taught me and my preferred method still. I wouldn't bother with the bridle either. Old Kitt was so sweet and gentle

I could guide her with my knees and a hackamore.

We were under way in no time without a lick of trouble, which confirmed my already-low opinion of Nat and Ol as watchmen. Our way was lit by the remains of a generous gibbous moon and the air had a sweet, fresh smell, like a barrel of apples. Kitt stepped lively, her eyes bright and her ears forward and rabbity. Earl Smith trotted alongside full of doggy purpose, determined to achieve our shared goal, whatever it was.

We were more than a mile down the road before I remembered Pa's shotgun. The realization I had left it behind struck me like a blow to the chest. I raised my eyes to the once-friendly moon and cursed myself for a fool. From that moment forward the woods lining the road looked a little darker, the September air felt a little colder. Was that something moving in the bramble by the butternut trees? I shook my head and dealt Kitt a hard kick in the ribs, undeserved. She turned her head toward me, showing an indignant eye.

Reluctantly she picked up the pace, but the closer we got to Hi's place, the more nervous I felt. Something was wrong. Hi was an early riser; I should have been seeing chimney smoke by then and I didn't. When we got to the turnoff, Kitt stopped altogether. She sensed something too. We stood motionless, companions in dread, looking down the dark road that led to Hi's farmhouse. The road was a fine macadam, its crushed stone surface pearly gray in the moonlight. Poor Hi, he toiled like a field slave on that road one whole summer just to please his Eastern wife, who was always complaining about Missouri dust. Then she up and left him anyhow.

Me and Kitt stood frozen, listening. The nigras said horses can see a ghost, and if a rider drops down low and looks between a horse's ears, the rider can see it too. I got down on Kitt's neck and peered between her hairy ears. I didn't see any apparition but that didn't mean it wasn't there. Should we turn around and go back? Earl Smith did not seem concerned, but this was cold comfort. I respected his animal knowing, yet I would have preferred a human opinion at the time. Finally I chose to go on. The sky was brightening and the birds were tuning up in the cottonwoods down by the river. I'd come all this way for a lemon and I guess I'd get one.

Obedient to my wishes, Kitt started slowly along the macadam. Fifty yards down the road we rounded a curve. There was Hi's farmhouse, quiet as a tomb in the gray light. The front door was hanging open like a mouth, and stuff was strewn all over the place, on the porch and in the yard. I saw broken chairs and dishes, clothing and bedding hanging from the rails, the Eastern wife's china cabinet sideways on the ground with its contents smashed and tossed about like bits of broken bone. Hi's prized grandfather clock lay face down on the porch steps, lifeless as a corpse.

"Uncle Hi? It's me, Hattie Rood!"

My words echoed back, and again I rebuked myself for a fool. What was I thinking? Whoever did this might still be around! I held my breath and braced for a rush of murderous shadows.

No one answered, nothing moved.

Kitt kept turning, wanting to go home. I did too, but we couldn't. What if Hi was lying hurt somewhere, waiting and praying for someone to help him? What if he was watching me that very instant but couldn't call out on account of his injuries? I figured I owed him for the Bledsoes and his many other kindnesses. I slid to the ground, keeping hold of Kitt's rope, and led her toward the house. She nickered but there was no answer from the barn. The only living thing was one white chicken pecking in the yard.

I looped Kitt's rope around the porch rail and walked through the open door, stepping on broken glass as I did so. The parlor was topsy-turvy. What little furniture remained inside was smashed to smithereens. Same in the kitchen and downstairs bedroom.

"Hi?"

Still no answer. My fear was less now. I was fairly sure

the marauders, whoever they were, were gone. Even so I climbed the stairs on tiptoe to check the upstairs bedrooms. All were mussed and empty. Of Uncle Hi I found no sign. I was outdoors on my way to the summer kitchen when Earl Smith started making a commotion over by the barn.

Slowly, certain nothing good was about to happen, I walked to the place where Earl was scratching and lunging at something sticking out of the ground. I couldn't figure out what I was looking at. Then I recognized two gray feet with a pair of hickory whips tied round the ankles. Whoever this was, he had been dragged to his grave alive; claw marks scored the earth on either side of the drag line. It had to be Hi Braddock. He was a tall, spare fellow, and those bony feet with toes long as fingers could not belong to anyone else. I felt vomit rising bitter in my throat and forced it back with deep breaths of cold air. I was thus engaged when Ol Shepherd rode up behind me. He scared me so, I got hiccups.

"Who's that?" he said, nodding at the feet.

"Like you care. His name was Hiram Braddock, and he was a good man."

Was Ol truly innocent, or play acting? This could well have been the work of bushwhackers, and Ol might have been one of them.

"Was he Northern or Southern?" Ol said.

"He walked the line," I said. Hi was Northern in his sympathies but only his friends knew that. "He proclaimed no allegiance."

Ol grunted.

"That means he was a Yank, in which case he got what he deserved." He spat on the grave. "Guess it's all up for you, brother Hiram! No more fried chicken and pecan pie for Sunday dinner, no Saturday night poker with the boys!"

I did not appreciate this levity at Hi's expense.

"Like I said, he was a good man. Better than you, Ol Shepherd! He surely did not deserve to die like this."

"Well, looks like someone thought different. Now get on

your horse. We're going back to the farm."

I pointed to Hi's gray feet sticking out of the ground like an obscene pair of mushrooms.

"We can't leave him for the wolves and catamounts," I said. "It ain't Christian."

Ol threw back his head and laughed, the first real laugh I'd heard from him in all the weeks I'd known him.

"Christian! Where you been, girl? Ain't nothing Christian about none of this! Get on that horse right now or I'll hogtie you and throw you on."

As I had no choice I did like he said. We rode side-by-side on the empty road under a red morning sky. When we were halfway the distance, it finally occurred to Ol to ask what I was doing at Hi Braddock's at that hour, dressed like I was. I'd been expecting the question but had not yet thought up a good answer.

"I don't have to tell you nothing," I said.

He shrugged.

"Maybe not, but you're going to have to do some explaining to somebody."

I thought I knew who he meant.

"That's not your nevermind. I'll worry about Pa."

"I ain't talking about your Pa. I mean Jesse. He's the one sent me. He thought maybe you was going for the Feds."

Ol's words hit me like a kick in the stomach. How could Jesse possibly think such a thing after all we'd been through? All we meant to each other?

"I don't believe you," I said. "Jesse trusts me. He knows I wouldn't do that."

Ol gave me a sideways look under his hat. It was too dark to see his face plain but I didn't have to. I could feature his smirk.

"Why would I make it up?" he said.

"Meanness." It was all I could come up with.

Ol laughed. At least someone was enjoying himself this dreary morning.

"Girl, if you think I'm mean, you don't know what mean is."

Didn't I though? I would like someone to please tell me what sixteen-year-old girl on God's green earth could know more about meanness than me. Hellfire! Hadn't I just seen a first-rate display of it in one poor man's feet with whips round the ankles?

We rode in silence then, each lost in solitary contemplation. As we neared the farm, Ol said, "Jesse James, he is a rare one. Bill Anderson and Archie Clement, they think highly of him. Fletch Taylor does, too. Me, I like Jesse well enough, but I prefer Frank's company. Jesse's smart though. I'll give him that. I believe he's the sort who would make a good politician."

"Meaning what?"

"Well, he's the sort who starts with ten and makes it twenty. And he comes out smellin' like a rose ever time. I ain't criticizing, mind. I'm just saying."

"Shut your gob hole, Ol Shepherd," I said. "I ain't interested."

Chapter Seventeen

Pa and Doak waited for us on the porch. Doak was relieved to see me but Pa stood like a statue, arms folded across his bony chest, his face like thunder. We rode up to the house. I dismounted and tied Kitt's lead to the rails.

Nothing would be gained by waiting for questions, so I jumped right in.

"Hi Braddock is dead, Pa. I went over to his place this morning to borrow something and I found him. His place is all smashed up and he is dead."

Doak banged his crutch on the floor in anger but Pa showed no reaction.

"Uncle Hi dead?" Doak said. "Hattie, are you sure?"

"I saw a grave. It was Hi's—it had to be."

"Who did it?" Doak said. "Federals? Bushwhackers?"

He glared at Ol, still in the saddle behind me.

"Don't look at me," Ol said. "I don't know nothin' about it. I followed her over there because Jesse said to!"

"What were you doing?" Pa said. "Are those Ben's clothes?"

I explained about the cake and the lemon. Even though it was the truth it sounded lame to my own ears.

"I didn't mean to make trouble," I said. "I wanted the cake to be a surprise—I thought I'd be back before anyone noticed."

I embarrassed myself by starting to cry, and once the hot tears commenced I could not stop them. I carried on for a bit; when I pulled myself together, Pa's face was twisted up in a way I hadn't seen since Ben died.

"You wanted to surprise me with a cake?" His voice was thick.

Then I remembered. Pa's birthday was next week! This was a most fortuitous circumstance—he thought I was making it for him! Oh, what vain creatures men were, and how easily misled! I didn't like myself for it but, just like with Joe, I'd let Pa think what he wanted if it served my purpose.

"Yes, Pa, a Jenny Lind cake, like I made for Doak that time. I remembered how much you liked it and I wanted to surprise you for your birthday."

Pa came down from the porch and for an instant I thought he meant to embrace me, something he had not done since I could not remember when. But if that was his intention he resisted it. Instead he went to the rail and untied Kitt's rope.

"Doak and me will ride over to see about Hiram," he said. "If we're not back in an hour, get over to Fritz Heizinger's place and fill him in. He'll take care of you." Like I needed someone to do that!

Pa and Doak had to ride double on Kitt, since Ol would not make them the loan of his horse. Once they were gone I went inside and sank down on Ma's horsehair settee, exhausted and overcome with disgust for all humankind—myself included.

"Well, aren't you the smooth liar, Hattie Rood? I wouldn't have thought it of you."

Jesse came into the parlor and sat on the chair opposite me. He looked fresh and rested in the bright morning sun with his long hair wet and combed back from his face. There was a white spot of soap left over from shaving, just below his right ear.

He looked so handsome, I became uncomfortably aware of my own appearance. My hair was half down, and Ben's pants had come unrolled and piled up on my shoes.

"I don't lie," I said.

"No?" He smiled. "You were going to make that cake for me, weren't you?"

"No. It was for Pa." He appeared so pleased with himself, I wanted to deny him satisfaction.

His smiled deepened. "I was born at night, Hattie," he said, "but not last night."

Now I was mad. The things that happened that morning were nothing to smile about, what with Hi dead and who knew what to come. And I had not forgotten what Ol said, about Jesse's suspicions of me. That was a deep cut. He saw the anger building in me.

"Now, don't get mad, Hattie," he said. "You found out it was my birthday a while back and you wanted to do something special for me because you are a sweet girl. Why, there's nothing wrong with that. I like sweet girls."

I hopped to my feet.

"If I'm so sweet why did you send that weasel Ol Shepherd to spy on me?"

His blue eyes widened.

"I didn't. I just wanted to make sure you didn't get into trouble, Hattie. That's all. Why would you think I sent him to spy?"

He walked to me, stopping just inches away. I smelled his shaving cream, his clean, sun-dried clothes. He took my chin between his thumb and forefinger and tipped my head up so our eyes met. My heart was pounding.

"Why would you think that?" he said again.

"Because Ol said that. He said you thought I was going to the Yankees to rat you out."

He smiled.

"Who do you believe? Me or Ol Shepherd?"

Then he leaned down and kissed me. I'd been kissed before, more than once, by Joe and others, but never like this. I felt altogether transported out of myself. I wanted it to last forever.

"Do you trust me, Hattie?" he said.

I nodded my head and told myself I meant it. But deep down inside where my truest self lived, I felt a cold draught of doubt.

Chapter Eighteen

Tobacco is a beautiful crop in the growing stage and a money-maker at the end, but only if the farmer is skilled, the weather cooperates, and the market is friendly. Therefore our prospects were chancy.

Pa planted the Yellow Orinoco variety, which was well-suited to the rich black soil of our land. Though he did not use tobacco himself, and forbade his sons to use it also, Pa chose this leaf because it was said to have a sweet property most desired by chewers. Popularity of the fine-cut chewing leaf was on the rise across the country, Pa said, and would be in great demand from European buyers, too, after the war. I didn't know anything about international commerce, but I loved the look of our fields, especially in the fall; in September, when the ripening leaves changed from dark green to spotted and yellow. It was important that they not be allowed to over-ripen to a solid yellow, for if that happened it would be impossible to cure the leaf to the bright fancy color which was most prized.

But fall was also a hard time for the tobacco grower, for it was the season when the stalks were split and cut, tied in bunches on sticks, and hung on the scaffold. If the weather was good it was hung outdoors, for the sun-dried product produced a softer and more beautiful color, and a chewer will not countenance a tobacco that has the least hint of a smoky, fire-cured flavor. When the leaves were thoroughly spotted, the scaffolds were carried to the curing barn to finish until November, when they went to the stripping shed for sorting and grading. Thus a grower would not see his money till December, when the crop was taken to Camden for final grading, purchase and, God willing, shipping.

Doak did his best to help Pa with the harvest, but his leg was slow healing and he wasn't much use in the field. The scoundrels Nat and Ol made themselves scarce during the day, except at meal times, but Jesse offered to pitch in, saying he wanted to repay our hospitality and the work would help make him strong again. Nat, in his usual sour fashion, complained that if Jess was healed enough to cut tobacco, he was healed enough to return to Anderson's camp. But Jesse was firm.

"I owe this much to Captain Rood and I'm staying till the work's done."

Even Pa had to acknowledge he was a valuable hand, having tended his mother's tobacco fields in Clay County before taking to the bush. I enjoyed watching him working shirtless in the hot sun, muscles under brown skin. He threw himself into the work whole-hog, but kept a pistol tucked in his belt at all times. Yet even with his assistance Pa still was shorthanded. I volunteered myself one morning at breakfast.

"Let me, Pa. I know how to cut and stake. I've seen it done."

At first he would not hear of it.

"I ain't sunk so low I'd see my own daughter sweating in the field like a nigra! What would people say?"

I did not give a fig about that, but Pa could not abide such abandon in a female.

"My good name's all I got left," he said. "I ain't about to let that go."

But as the days passed hot and dry and leaves ripened on the stalk, he swallowed his pride.

"Hattie, I reckon I'll be needing you after all." The words cut his mouth like sharpened wire. "But if anybody comes, hunker down. Don't let nobody see."

My job was to protect the cut plants from sunburn. I did this by following Jess, Doak, and Pa through the rows, piling ten or twelve plants together and turning them over on the side of the hill, leaf covered, stalk to the sun. I was very happy at this work and much preferred it to housekeeping. The best part was being alongside Jesse, spending every moment with him: breathing the same air, smelling the same smells, sharing the same small triumphs and tragedies. It was what I wanted to do every day for the rest of my life.

One afternoon we cut away for a while, just the two of us, to walk down by the river. Pa and Doak were occupied in the barn. Me and Jess figured we were due a break. It was hot, the air so wet and heavy it felt like an actual weight on the head and shoulders. The cicadas were buzzing loud and steady and I felt transported. We walked so close together, my shoulder bumped against his arm. When we reached the riverbank, he took my hand and we sat on a fallen log. The water sparkled in the sunlight, dusted with diamonds. Happy and peaceful, I wanted him to kiss me like he did in the parlor.

He didn't though. Instead he asked me if I'd gotten over that thing Ol said, about him not trusting me.

"I suppose. It bothered me though. I need my friends to be honest with me."

"I'm honest with you," he said. "Ask me anything. I'll tell you the truth."

Oh, there was so much I wanted to know! First and foremost, had he been with a girl before? I bet he had. And if so, who was she? Not the Sue he mentioned in his early ravings. She—I had since learned to my considerable relief—was his sister. But was there someone? Maybe a Clay County girl, who were said to be wild? How had it happened? Did he still have feelings for her? Was she pretty as me?

"No," I said, lowering my eyes. "There's nothing."

Chapter Nineteen

Doak took over the weekly trips to Richmond for groceries and mail. This was chancy in case someone recognized him and ratted him out to the Yankees, but he said he had to go as it wasn't safe for a woman to travel alone, and that was true enough. I suspected an equal reason was he needed a break from the fieldwork on account of his leg was not healing right. I saw pain every time I looked at him, right there in his tired eyes and bony face. Nobody said it out loud, but if he didn't start mending soon we would have to find him a doctor. They were expensive and often did more harm than good, but if infection settled in the bone—well, none of us wanted to contemplate the consequences of that.

Evenings, me, Doak and Jesse repaired to the porch for Jesse's reading of the newspapers, which he read out loud by lamplight. He was a halting reader but a determined one. I sensed he was touchy about his subscription school education and a touch resentful that Frank's schooling was superior to his own. Despite this, or maybe because of it, Jesse enjoyed imparting knowledge. Me, I just liked the sound of his voice, which was soothing and melodious and altogether pleasing to the ear. I'd lie back in my chair, stroking Earl's ears, wishing Doak would go inside so I could have more of Jesse's kisses.

But reading those newspapers put Jesse in no mood for kissing. War news and politics got him more worked up than

I did. Naturally the Unionist ones riled him most of all as they were boastful of Northern victories and of these there were plenty. Lately they were rapturous about Sherman's taking of Atlanta, which was big news indeed, and Little Phil Sheridan's ruination of the Shenandoah Valley. This was a beautiful place, or so I'd heard, with blue-green forests and lush sweetgrass meadows full of wildflowers. Of course I'd never been there, I'd never been out of Missouri, but my people lived in Virginia before they moved to Kentucky before they moved here, so I felt a kinship with those Virginia folks Jesse read about. They were living through the same bad business we were here in Missouri, at the hand of the same oppressor.

Still, much as I hated the Yankees, my passion was nothing compared to Jesse's and those Unionist papers only fanned the flames. He called the Union generals every hard name he could think of, though he never used a cuss word. And it wasn't only war news that fired him up; Jesse was also very radical in his politics. Me, I never gave much thought to politics; for one, women won't never be able to vote, not in my lifetime, and two, politics was nothing but gas anyhow. In our times, when such discussions were like as not settled with the business end of a pistol, what good was it? Jesse, though, held otherwise. Like the night he read in the *Weekly Union* that Sherman's capture of Atlanta made Lincoln's re-election in November likely and that even Northern Democrats were leaning toward Black Abe and the drunken Tennessee traitor, Johnson. That made Jesse real hot.

"Democrats for Lincoln! Is that what Democrats in the North have sunk to? Well, I am a Democrat! I am a Missouri Democrat and I tell you sure as I'm sitting here any Democrat votes for 'Ape' Lincoln best not show his Copperhead face in west Missouri or his sins will find him out! Lincoln won't never be my president—that is played out!"

Doak said if he felt so strong about it then why didn't he join the regular Confederate army and fight the Union proper?

"I'm going back with Price soon as my leg heals," Doak

said. "Come with me, why don't you?"

But Jesse was not interested. He told us a story then I had not heard before, of the time Federal soldiers came to his mother's farm in Clay County, looking for Frank. They didn't find Frank, but they found Jesse out in the fields plowing. The bluebellies put a rope around his neck and drug him through the dirt. They kicked him and hit him with their fists and sabers, but he wouldn't give Frank up.

"I told them they could put me through, but I wouldn't never give up Frank and the boys," he said, remembering. I believed him too, every word.

The boys' stepfather, Reuben Samuel, their mother's third husband, was treated even worse. They strung the old man up, waited till he was near dead then cut him down, once, twice, three times, before finally giving up and leaving him hanging from a tree, a meal for the flesh-eaters. Jesse's mother, Zerelda, took him down.

"He ain't never been the same, though," Jess said touching his head. "Not up here. He's mostly a child."

Me and Doak considered this sorrowful story.

"So, I'll fight with Price when he comes," Jesse said, "and I'll ride to hell and back with Jo Shelby any day, but I will not tie up official with the regulars. You said it yourself, Doak, Jeff Davis don't give a fig for Missouri! We can go to pie for all he cares, him and all them in Richmond. Just look what he did to Price and his boys, sending 'em down to fight in Mississippi while Missouri was left to the Feds! No, me and Frank ride together and we ride with Bill Anderson."

I tried to turn the conversation away from this dreary war talk to topics of interest to me, like the story of the Mayfield sisters, Sallie and Jennie, who served the bushwhackers as spies and couriers and sometimes even rode with them. I greatly esteemed the Mayfields and their adventurous ways! Earlier this summer the girls were caught with a band of guerillas near Montevallo and sent to Gratiot, the dreaded women's prison in St. Louis, where the Federals confined and mistreated women suspected of aiding the rebels. But the Mayfields escaped! How, accounts differ. Could be they bribed their male guards with gold and went over the wall, could be they enticed them with something else. Me, I admired them either way. A woman ought not suffer abuse without putting up resistance and she is entitled, way I see it, to use all the tools at her disposal. After all, that's why the good Lord gave them to her. Anyhow, I pointed out a story in the *Caucasian* saying they had not been recaptured; but Doak and Jess weren't interested. Jesse, still boiling about that election business, left us to join Nat and Ol at their camp in the woods. I watched him disappear into the trees with some disappointment, having hoped for a different kind of evening.

"Why the sour face?" Doak said. I could tell from his smile that he already knew the answer so I didn't supply one.

"I saw Joe Craighead in town today," Doak went on. "He asked about you."

Joe. The mention of his name weighed me down like a long coat of wet wool. I had not thought of Joe for a while and I didn't want to now. It made me feel bad about myself.

"Well, how is he?" I said because Doak expected it.

"He seems all right. Hannah McFaddin was there, shopping so she said, though mostly making eyes at Joe. She didn't much like it, him asking after you."

Ha! I had to smile at that. I bet she didn't!

"Well I'm not surprised," I said. "Hannah set her bonnet for Joe ever since you and her parted ways."

I felt Doak's eyes on me, trying to measure my true feelings. If he was expecting the green-eyed monster, she did not rise to the bait.

"Poor Hannah," I said. "What happened with you and her anyhow? You never said."

I didn't truly expect an answer, but Doak surprised me.

"What happened was I met another girl, Sarah, down in Arkansas. It was a dilemma for me. I debated with myself back and forth—Hannah or Sarah, Sarah or Hannah—but finally I wrote and told Hannah it was off between us. I felt bad because we had an understanding, you could say, but it was the right thing. I'm going back to Arkansas for Sarah. We're going to get married."

"Why, Doak, I'm real happy for you." I was, too. I never liked Hannah McFaddin. "What's she like?"

"She's got red hair, like you, only she's pretty and sweet-tempered."

I made a face at him. "Well, thank you very much." He smiled.

"But that's not what I want to talk about now."

I sensed a lecture coming on, no doubt concerning my personal circumstances. I got up and said I needed to uncover the soft water barrels since it looked like rain tonight. It was true; the wind was pushing wispy silvery clouds fast across the sky. But Doak told me to sit down and I did like he said. He was still my favorite brother.

"I know what's happening with you and Jesse," he said. "Not the particulars of it but enough."

I puffed up in protest. He raised his hand.

"Stop it. Just hear me out. I'm not casting blame. I couldn't hardly do that, could I, seeing what I just told you about me and Hannah? As for Jesse, I like him too. I didn't expect to, seeing as how he's a 'whacker and he and them other two were putting you and Pa in danger, but he has an agreeable nature. Still, it won't work with you and him. You think it will, but it won't. Settling down, tending a family, those things won't hold him. Some men set their sights on a larger portion and Jesse James is one. I know, I've seen it before."

"Are you finished?"

Why was everyone so sure they knew what was right for me, better than I did?

"No. You better make things right with Joe Craighead before it's too late. Hannah McFaddin can be mighty persuasive when she's of a mind to."

I knew what that meant. I wouldn't put it past her.

"I don't care. She can have him." A thought struck me. "I suppose Pa put you up to this?"

Doak shook his head. "No, Hattie. It's just me talking to you tonight and I hope you listen."

I thanked him for his concern and excused myself to open the rain barrels. It was the last conversation me and my brother would ever have.

Chapter Twenty

The militia came that night, right after the rain stopped. The evening sky was bright and clear of clouds, the air cool and fresh. I woke at midnight from a heavy sleep to the sound of horsemen in the yard, calling out the men of the house.

"Come out!" The Yankee's voice was loud and booming, like a brimstone preacher's. "Come out, old man! It's not you we want, Captain, but that Secesh boy of yours. I got someone here wants to see him."

This brought a chorus of laughter. I peered out the corner of my bedroom window and saw a dozen blue-uniformed men in the moonlight. One wore a rope coiled around his shoulder.

I ran across the hall to Doak's room. He was already out of bed and dressed, pulling on his boots.

"Where are you going?" I said.

"Out the window. I'll try for the woods."

From below there came a battering on the door. Pa yelled at the Yankees to go away.

"My boy ain't here!" he shouted. "I don't know where he is!"

"We seen him, Captain! We seen him in town. Now send him out, old man, or we'll come in and get him!"

I wondered about Jesse, as he had not returned to the loft that evening. Was he in the woods with Nat and Ol? Would they help us out?

As Doak put his leg through the window, we heard the sound of breaking glass below. He climbed out and onto the sloping roof, keeping low. But the Yankees must have expected this, for no sooner was he out there than the bullets started flying.

"Doak! Come back!"

I leaned out the window to pull him in.

"No Hattie!" He turned and stood, trying to push me back into the room. "Get away from the window!"

A bullet struck him in the chest, spinning him in a half-circle, then another bullet, then another. Each time I heard the thunk of lead striking meat, and each time a black blossom of blood appeared on Doak's white linen shirt as he staggered and turned and tried to reclaim his footing on the wooden shingles. Time slowed to a crawl as I watched him topple backward, windmilling his arms, closer and closer to the edge. Our eyes met in one frozen moment of horror and disbelief before he disappeared over the side.

I stood still, shocked, not believing what was happening. Somewhere distant a woman screamed, a sound shrill as a steam whistle, grating, insistent. Time passed before I realized the screaming woman was me. I squeezed my head between my hands, trying to reclaim my senses. Then I heard Pa yelling downstairs and ran pell-mell to join him.

He was in the parlor with his shotgun trained on the door. The battering had stopped. The windows on either side of the door were broken, and Ma's lacy white curtains blew in the September breeze. Glass littered the floor and the horse-hair settee. It was crazy, but I thought how upset Ma would be to see this muss in her company room.

"Pa!" I said. "They shot Doak! They shot him off the roof! We got to go to him!"

Blood drained from Pa's face. He said, "They shot him? They shot Doak? Is he...?"

I knew what he meant and I was pretty sure I knew the answer, but I could not say the word either.

"I don't know, Pa—I don't know! We got to go to him!"

He ran from the parlor to the kitchen, stopping at the door. When I tried to follow, he pushed me back.

"I may have lost my last son tonight," he said. "Don't you go giving me any more to grieve about."

I said I wouldn't, but as soon as Pa was out the back door I went out the front. I wasn't about to hide under the bed like a ninny when all hell was breaking loose, when the only family I had left was up against it. I ran round the side of the house and saw Pa and the Yankees out back. They were standing round Doak's still body, his shirt starkly white on the dark ground.

"We didn't come out here to kill your boy, Captain Rood," one of the Yankees said, "but he was fixing to run. He oughtn't have done that."

"God damn you!" Pa's voice was terrible to hear. "You did come to kill him you miserable son-of-a-bitch and now you have! You Yankees killed both my boys! God damn you to hell!"

I sank to the ground, a human puddle of misery and heartbreak. What had we Roods done to bring this unending calamity down upon us? How had we offended? At that awful moment a question came to me, forming up in my mind like an image from the Old Testament. Could this be punishment for the things our Missouri granddaddies did to the Mormons all those years ago? Could it be the Danites weren't crazy after all and these, our current trials, were their heaven-sent retribution?

"What should we do with the old man, captain?" a second Yankee said. "Should we take him in for harboring a enemy soldier? Him and the girl too?"

Girl! They knew about me! I jumped to my feet. I wasn't going to no Yankee prison! No Gratiot for me—I would run! I would live off the land like the Mayfield sisters! But what about Pa? How could I leave him? And Earl Smith? Where was that dog anyhow? I was torn, calculating my options, when a movement in the woods caught my eye. It was a man, crouching in the undergrowth, raising a rifle to his shoulder to take aim. Hellfire! I never thought I'd be glad to see Nat Tigue, but surely I was!

Boom! The gun went off loud as a cannon and sent those Yankees running for their horses and every which way. Boom! Boom! One of the bluebellies dropped mid-stride, hitting the ground like a side of beef. The others flew right by. One even jumped over him, too concerned with his own scaly hide to give their fallen comrade a helping hand. Hell, make room for one more!

Now I saw more flashes of gunfire from the woods, Jesse and Ol I figured. The Yanks jumped on their horses, sending random pistol shots toward the trees. Cowards that they were, they took to the road at top speed while I ran round back of the house. There was Pa sitting on the ground holding Doak's limp body. I walked toward them, terror mounting with every step, dreading what I was about to see.

"Pa?"

He raised his head to me. His face was wet with tears and his mouth was hanging open.

"Pa?" I walked to him and put my hand on his shoulder. Doak's eyes were open, staring at the starry sky, but he didn't see it.

"My boy," Pa said. "My boy."

Pa valued his sons above all; I knew that all along. They helped him build his barn, they worked alongside him in the fields, they fought his wars. Now I was all he had left. I might not be a boy, but I was something.

"You've still got me, Pa," I said. "I'm still here."

He looked at me without comprehension.

"I shouldn't have let him go into town," he said. "I knew somebody would turn him in. I should've stopped him."

Unspoken in this was that Doak went in place of me, because the roads were too dangerous for a girl. Unspoken in this was it should have been me and not Doak.

"I'm sorry, Pa."

Jesse, Ol, and Nat arrived, guns in hand. They didn't say anything. The scene required no words.

"I'm sorry for your loss, Captain," Jesse said. "Doak was a good man. I liked him very much. It's terrible what the Yankees have done to you and your family. It's unforgivable."

Pa looked at him blankly, like he was not really hearing what Jesse said.

"Me and the boys will help you bury him and we best do it now. Then you and Hattie have to get out of here, Captain. Those Yanks will be back."

"Where will we go?" I said.

"Don't you have kinfolk around? Somebody who'll take you in?"

I thought of Joe, of all the times he'd offered his home to us. That was no longer an option. Also Fritz Heizinger, but that was the first place the Yankees would look, plus we would put him in danger.

"No," I said. "There's no one."

Jesse ran a hand through his hair.

"Then you'll have to come with us to Anderson's camp. All right, Captain Rood?"

Pa's eyes were glassy and he looked very strange, not like himself at all. Jesse looked at me.

"Pa?" I said. "Should we go to the bushwhacker's camp?"

We stood there in the silver moonlight, and I saw us like figures in an old-time painting, gathered around an old man, cradling his dead son in his arms.

"Take your Pa inside, Hattie," Jesse said. "We'll bury your brother. Meantime, pack your things—your Pa's too—but not much. We'll travel light."

Chapter Twenty-one

We rode for hours, through dark woods and across streams and valleys. I left without Earl, an act of betrayal on my part that pained me like a dagger to my heart. It bothered me that he had not barked when the bluecoats showed up. It did not auger well for his current condition.

We rode in an easterly direction till the dawn star rose and still we rode on. Nat and Ol led the way, sharing a horse like a couple of sour old maids. Pa followed on Kitt while me and Jesse brought up the rear on Nat's bay.

Despite the circumstances I enjoyed my prolonged closeness to Jesse, the smell of him and the warmth of his body next to mine. Was it wrong of me to feel such things with my brother not yet cold in his grave? It did not feel wrong. Maybe God or nature or whoever was in charge of such things showed mercy by providing a blanket of numbness to the beleaguered soul whose portion of grief exceeded his or her capability. One look at Pa, though, threw that philosophy into question. He wore his pain like a gray mask of suffering. So lost was he in his misery he was not even aware of his surroundings.

We did not reach the bushwhacker camp till mid-morning, and then we were on it in an instant, emerging from the woods onto a scene of enterprise and activity. The air smelled of cook fires and coffee and frying meat. Socks and blankets dried on the skeletal limbs of autumnal bushes. Two men came forward to meet us. One was Jim, the fellow who accompanied Frank to our house the night they brought Jesse. The other was small and slight, so tiny I at first mistook him for a child. Although I could not place him, he was somehow familiar and the association was not a pleasant one. Jesse, however, greeted this little man with especial fondness.

"Archie!" Jesse slid to the ground to embrace him, towering over his little friend like a big, broad-shouldered mountain. As the small man's gray eyes took me in over Jesse's shoulder, I all at once remembered where I had seen him before. He was one of the bushwhackers who came to my rescue on the Richmond road the day Cy was killed. He was the one who shot the Yankee officer and then freed him of his ears.

"Where's Buck?" Jesse said, scanning the bearded faces for his brother's long mug.

Archie said Frank and some others had gone to Rocheport to collect taxes.

"Contributory taxes, for the support and maintenance of our company," Archie said to me, "and voluntary, too. Bill don't pressure no one to contribute. That's Bill Anderson, I'm talking about, in case you don't know."

If he was trying to goad from me a reaction to the infamous name, I denied him satisfaction. With a wink Jess lifted me down from the horse. Only then, when he set me on the ground, did I realize the camp had gone quiet; even the squirrels had ceased their busy chatter. All eyes were on me, measuring my worth from head to toe, like I was a horse they might buy, or a cow.

"What's wrong with you boys?" Jesse said with mock astonishment. "Ain't you seen a pretty girl before? Or maybe it's her red hair got you all standing around with your mouths open!"

"What are we going to do with her, Jess?" Jim said. "This ain't no place for a woman."

Jesse's arm tightened around my shoulders.

"I know it. But I had to bring her. Her farm wasn't safe neither. That's her old man, over there. There's something wrong with him." He pointed to Pa, who sat on Kitt, lost in his own dark world. "They took me in when I was hurt and now I aim to return the favor. Just for a bit. It ain't permanent."

I walked over to Pa and put my hand on his leg. "Come down," I said, "I'll find us something to eat." The face looking down at me was a death's head. His jaw was slack and his eyes sunk back in his head like two holes burnt in a blanket. I had never seen him so.

Jess and me finally got Pa down off the horse. I was surprised and upset to see Pa had pissed himself. Jess pretended not to notice and went off to talk business with Cummins while another bushwhacker helped me find Pa clean clothes and a blanket and get him settled in by a fire. Pa rolled over on his side and fell asleep right off.

"What's the matter with him?" the bushwhacker said. He was a strong, round-shouldered farm boy with ginger-colored hair and freckled skin. The others called him Hamp Watts. Maybe because he reminded me of Joe, I trusted him instantly.

"Feds came to our house and killed my brother last night. Pa ain't been right since."

Hamp nodded in sympathy.

"How old is your Pa?"

I never thought of this and had to do some ciphering. He was born in eighteen and twenty.

"He is forty-four."

Hamp nodded again, like my answer had a sad meaning for him.

"Same as my Pa," he said.

For some reason I wanted this Hamp Watts to know my father once was more than what he saw now.

"Pa fought the Mexican War," I said. "That's how we got our farm in Ray County. The government gave it to him in answer for his brave service."

Hamp said his pa got his place in Johnson County the same way.

Jesse went on talking with Jim Cummins and the other bushwhackers, and I got the feeling they were talking about us. I could tell from the looks I was getting they did not want us there. Jesse must have made a good argument on our behalf, though, because me and Pa got to stay. It was a good thing too because we were beat down, Pa especially. We hung around camp all day, not doing anything. I tried to sleep and every now and then I'd doze off, but each time I was jolted awake by my own nervousness. I was too wrought up to relax, even though Jess and Hamp stayed close by. I kept expecting a party of Feds to come crashing through the bush.

The bushwhackers stayed busy, cleaning and oiling guns, tending their horses, frying up salt pork and drinking coffee. Hamp smoked tobacco and Jess chewed, something I'd not seen him do before. Jesse seemed nervous, anxious for his brother to get back. His clear blue eyes were constantly moving, scanning the trees, fixing on any little sound. Always he blinked a lot—he told me his mother said he had granulated eyelids, though neither of us knew exactly what that meant— and whenever he was tired or nervous he blinked even more. Such was the case now.

Though I could not sleep, Pa did nothing but. He slept all day long and into the night. It got cold and I covered him with two blankets, his and the one Jess found for me. We'd left the house with practically nothing, only the few things I threw in Pa's canvas kit. There was one change of clothing for each of us, nothing more: no bedding, no coats, no underclothes. I brought only two dresses, the faded blue gingham I'd worn for the past two days and the equally tired red calico in Pa's kit. I wished for Ben's warm and serviceable old things, the clothes I wore the dreadful morning I found Hi's body. Was it only last week? It seemed a lifetime ago.

The bushwhackers provided me with the overcoat of a Federal officer. It smelled of its previous owner, a pipe smoker and user of hair dressing. The collar smelled of pomade I recognized, an Arabian macassar once sold in Craighead's dry goods store. I liked the smell of it, redolent as it was of a happier, more comfortable time.

Around midnight I was shaken from my fitful sleep by commotion at the edge of the camp where two men were wrestling with a third. Others joined in and the intruder was quickly subdued. Oh, the poor soul! I pitied him, whoever he was.

The victors dragged the unhappy stranger to the fireside and threw him to the ground at little Archie's feet. To my surprise, it was an Indian, dressed in a Union jacket, with long black hair hanging loose under a kepi. He wore a cavalryman's striped trousers tucked into soft, knee-high leather boots.

I had heard talk that the Yankees employed red Indians from the Kansas reservations as trackers and scouts, but until that moment I had not believed it. Why would the red man join hands with his oppressor? It seemed about as likely as a black man soldiering for the South, but then I heard accounts of this too. Curious, I joined the bushwhackers gathered round the Indian on the ground who glowered up at us with bold black eyes. I admired his lack of fear, although I was certain his fate would be a wretched one.

"He was watchin' us from up on the bluff top," one of the bushwhackers said, kicking the Indian as he spoke. "Some sorry kind of Injun, ain't he Arch? To let a farm boy like me get the drop on him!"

He raised his leg for another kick, but before he could deal it the Indian grabbed his attacker's boot and yanked his legs out from under him. The bushwhacker landed close to the fire, raising a shower of sparks. His comrades roared their appreciation at this unexpected turn of events.

"Well, Karl," Jesse said. "Maybe that Injun got some onions after all!"

Karl drew his pistol from his belt, thumbed back the hammer, and would have dispatched the Indian then and there had Archie not stopped him.

"Hold on. Let's see what our red friend has to tell us first."

Archie squatted down on his heels so he was eye-level with the Indian. I felt my skin crawl. Something awful was going to happen and I wanted no part of it. I'd had my fill of death and dying, thank you very much, sufficient to last me till the end of my days. I looked over to where Pa lay, still wrapped in his blanket. His eyes were open and turned toward the fire, watching the men hogtie the Indian, but showing no emotion. He may as well have been watching them skin a rabbit. There was something bad wrong with Pa, that was certain. Though never a soft man, he did have a sense of injustice, or used to. But he did not flinch at the injustice done to that Indian, not when Archie started laying burning embers on the man's skin, not when he put hot coals in his ears, not when he at last started screaming. Me, I could not listen to it and took off running into the woods, crashing through the scrub with my hands over my ears. I could not see where I was going in the darkness and fell more than once, yet each time I got up and kept on running till I couldn't hear the Indian's screams any more.

For the first time in what seemed like years, I found myself alone. I sat on a dead log, looking up at the starry sky. In the old days I might have prayed at such a moment, or made a wish, but no longer. Instead I studied the moon, a giant glowing orb of silver, wondering was it possible this same moon was looking down right now on our house, or what was left of it? Was it looking on Earl Smith, waiting for me to come for him? On Doak's new grave? Was this same moon shining on Last Chance Gulch in the Montana Territory, on gold glittering in icy snow-melt rivers, just waiting for me and Jess to come pick it up?

Someone was coming toward me and not trying to be quiet about it. I hoped it was Jesse and I guess every girl sometimes gets what she wishes for, because it was him. We sat together on the log for a time listening to a hoot owl close by.

"I want to go home," I said.

"I know it. It was wrong to bring you here, but I didn't know what else to do."

He put his arm around me and pulled me close. I relaxed completely, for what felt like the first time in years.

"I'll take you," he said.

Chapter Twenty-two

We left the bushwhacker camp at first light. They gave us food, oatcakes, and Federal saltpork to sustain us on our journey. Since Pa could not ride, Jess talked them out of a rickety buckboard light enough for Kitt to pull. I drove the buckboard and Jesse rode Nat Tigue's bay, though Nat did not make the loan of it graciously.

Jess was sorry to leave without seeing Frank, but he had promised to take me home and he made good on it. On the way out of camp we passed the Indian's head stuck on a sharpened stake, his bloodless face white as a fish's belly in the pale light. A bit beyond we came upon the body, hanging upside down by a single foot from the limb of a stout oak. Sickened though I was by these unholy objects, I could not look away. Why do men do such things to each other? What must God think of His creation now?

By mid-morning I was slumping on the bench, struggling to keep my eyes open. My lids felt heavy and raw, like they were lined with ground glass. The day grew warm, and I shed my Union overcoat. The sun on my back soothed my aching muscles. This comfort, along with the clop clop of Kitt's hoofs and the creak of her harness, conspired to lull me to sleep. Not even fear of Federal militia or freebooting highwaymen could keep me alert. I fought for wakefulness like a drowning swimmer striving for the surface. Oh, how I longed for my sweet bed back home, for the comfort of clean cotton sheets and my soft woolen blanket! I yearned to sleep, sleep, and sleep till all the heaviness was gone from my bones, but I might as well have wished myself the Queen of Sheba. I shook my head and pinched my cheeks and pushed on.

Every now and then Pa let out a moan. I didn't look at him because I couldn't do anything to help and he was pitiful to behold. What had happened to him? Was he laid low, maybe temporarily, by grief, or had he suffered a brain seizure like his sister, Auntie Sophronia? Auntie lived a long time after her affliction, although she never came back to herself. For the rest of her days she was fed, bathed, and diapered like a little baby. With all my soul, I prayed Pa would not be consigned to such a living purgatory.

At noon we stopped for a cold meal. We didn't dare make a fire, though I sorely wanted coffee. Jess did too, though he was not fuddled like me. After we ate he let me sleep a little, only forty-five minutes or so, but it helped. I could keep my eyes open then.

The wind picked up in the afternoon; the temperature dropped like a stone. Thunder rumbled and dead leaves swirled up around the horses' legs with a noise like a thousand rattlesnakes. I found myself remembering a story Ben read to me and Doak a long time ago about an Eastern schoolteacher who met up with a horseman in the dark autumn woods, a hellish horseman who had no head. The story scared me so bad I couldn't sleep for two nights after. Well, I would not have been too surprised to see that horseman that day.

A few minutes later Jesse spotted a cave in the limestone bluff above the dry creek bed we were following.

"Let's put up there," he said, scanning the low-hanging sky. "We're in for a blow, maybe a cyclone."

He got no argument from me. We concealed the horses and the buckboard in the scrub and scrambled up the hillside using rocks and branches to pull ourselves up. The slope was steep and heavy-going, but Jess was strong enough to carry

Pa on his back while I followed with blankets, water, and food. When we reached the top, we found Indian paintings on the smooth stone above the cave mouth. Jess and I studied them in the rising wind; there were crude drawings of animals and one manlike form with unnaturally long arms and legs and antler-like growths sticking out of his head. In some sheltered places the paint was still bright red, but mostly it had faded to a rusty orange, like a wagon wheel left out in the weather.

As we settled into the cave, the sky outside changed from slate gray to greenish-brown, like a ripening bruise.

"Yep, could be a cyclone," Jesse said, standing at the cave entrance. "That's what happened last time I saw a sky that color."

I tried to get Pa comfortable, making a pillow with one blanket and covering him with another. His eyes were on me the whole time, not blank as before but pleading.

"What is it, Pa?" I said. "Please tell me. Does something hurt you?"

He made a throaty sound but no words. I thought he might be thirsty so I raised him up and gave him water from the canteen. He took some, but most dribbled out the side of his mouth and down his chin.

"Don't worry Pa," I said, lowering his head on the pillow-blanket. "We're not far from home. Tonight you will sleep in your own bed and tomorrow I'll go to Richmond and find you a doctor."

Although I did not believe this, saying it could not hurt, not the way Pa was. Outside the cave entrance the wind was blowing louder than a steam locomotive. I sat beside Jesse on the hard dirt floor and together we watched nature unleash her fury. At first just leaves and twigs blew by, then as the wind picked up, branches and even small trees. The rain came, blowing hard and sideways, followed by hail, hard bullets of ice, some big as a pullet's egg. One such bounced into the cave and landed at Jesse's feet. He picked it up.

"Look at that. A stone that size would kill a man, if it hit him right. Crack his skull right open. Here, feel how hard and solid it is—like iron." He pressed the ice ball to my palm and wrapped my fingers around it. His hands were warm and wet from the melting ice; I thrilled to their touch, and thought about how they would feel on my skin.

The storm was roaring, uprooting or splitting giant trees and sending them crashing to earth. The sound was no longer that of a locomotive but of cannon fire, or as I imagined it. I backed deeper into the cave and covered my ears with my hands. Jesse came and held me against his chest. He smelled of woodsmoke and the lemon soap I washed his clothes in.

I felt better right off, the moment he touched me. There was something about him, a confidence or some other quality, that made you feel nothing bad could happen if he was there. No one else affected me that way, not before I met Jesse and not since. He wasn't much older than me, just a few months, but he was way beyond me along life's ladder of knowledge. He had an understanding of natural things and secrets of the heart I wouldn't have if I lived nine hundred sixty-nine years, like Methuselah. Jesse James was a rare kind of man, the kind other people were drawn to.

Jesse kissed me, not sweet and tender like before, but hard and insistent. He moved his mouth to the spot just below my ear—his breath hot and fast, raising gooseflesh on my skin. When Jesse's hand brushed across my breast and he started working on the buttons of my dress I felt the old, clear-headed Hattie wake up inside me. I let him get away with two or three buttons, and thus encouraged, he slid his hand under the fabric of my dress and onto my skin. I pushed him away, not because I wanted to, understand, but because it was right. Pa was there, for one, in body if not mind. Also, and maybe more important, I sensed Jesse expected it. He was not the sort to prize low-hanging fruit.

Turned out I was right. Dark as it was, I surely saw a glint of admiration in his eyes as he released me.

"I'm sorry, Hattie. Honest, I am. I guess I got beyond myself."

He turned and walked to the mouth of the cave where he stood with his back to me, a silhouette against the gray light of the storm, now beginning to subside. I redid my buttons, wondering when and how I could show Jesse the truth about me, about the kind I truly was. I could do it and I would—without disappointing him too—but the time would have to be just right.

I joined him, taking his hand, and he looked down at me and smiled.

"Last time I saw a storm like this was the day me and Ma took Frank over to Lexington for the loyalty oath. April 26, 1862. That's one day I won't never forget." Jesse spoke the words like they were made of wormwood.

"I bet you didn't know that, did you?" he said. "That Frank took the loyalty oath? Well, he did. It was right after the Yanks released him from being took prisoner. He'd just got back to the farm when the provost marshal sent a detail out saying they'd arrest him again unless he went with them to Liberty to take the oath and pay a fine. Me and Ma followed them to make sure nothing bad happened and we watched Frank take that oath. They made him proclaim his true allegiance to the United States government and pledge them his honor, property, and life, and sign a paper to that effect in a roomful of bluebellies. It made me sick, hearing Frank say them things. I couldn't hardly believe it. It's been two years and I still can't. Frank, the best and noblest boy I ever knew, and the Yanks turned him into a Percy man, the kind of man who sits down to piss."

I was shocked to hear him speak so harshly of Frank. Not only that, it was unfair. I rose to Frank's defense.

"He had to take that oath," I said. "Lots of people did it. It don't signify nothing."

Jesse looked at me like I'd just coughed up a hairball.

"Don't signify nothing! Hattie, it signifies everything. In the end, a man's word is all he's got and that's especially so for people like us Jameses, me and Frank, with no money or high social standing. I tell you this: I wouldn't never have said that oath, no matter what that provost marshal threatened to do to me. I still look up to Frank, I do, but not like before. Frank don't know how I feel, though. No one does. No one but you."

I understood then Jesse's hard streak ran deeper than I thought. He would not forget where a hatchet was buried.

But on the other hand, I liked what he said about the value of a man's word. A fellow who believed like that was unlikely to betray his marriage vows, and I was definitely starting to regard Jesse James of Clay County in a matrimonial way.

Chapter Twenty-three

In an hour the storm was over and we were back on the road. I thought maybe Jess would want to put up in the cave for the night, but when I suggested that, he determined to press on.

"Caves are a man trap," he said. "I couldn't never sleep in one. May as well bed down in a cage."

Our westward route followed an old Indian trail along the river, lined with loess bluffs on the far side and the river on the other. The trail ran through a dense stand of cottonwood, willow, and locusts whose seedpods rattled in the wind like a child's toy. In places the rain had turned the sandy soil to gumbo that stuck to the horses' feet with a sucking sound and sank the wagon wheels, thereby dramatically slowing our progress. But we continued through the night, stopping every few hours to rest the horses or drink from one of the many springs that trickled from the bluffs. The water was so cold it hurt your teeth, though it tasted strongly of minerals and was not nearly as sweet as our well at home. Home! Oh, what would we find there? Was there any home to return to?

My heart quickened as I began to spot familiar landmarks, recognizable even in darkness. There was the thicket where me, Ben, and Doak picked raspberries and fox grapes in the summer; there the riverbend where the sidewheeler

Tunis sank in 1841 while moving upstream with a load of woolen overcoats for soldiers on the frontier. Pa pointed the spot out to me and the boys one spring day.

"Every man and boy in these parts got himself a fine winter coat out of the deal," he said. "And we kept on finding them coats for years after, washing up downstream. They were still good, too, once you dried 'em out and got the mud off."

It hurt to remember Pa as he was then, when we were youngsters. I remembered him as wise, capable, and strong, a brave soldier. I looked at him now in the back of the buckboard, curled up on his side, wrapped in blankets. He was shrunken, small as a boy. In normal times, any one of the things that had befallen me lately—Doak's death, Pa's decline, Earl's disappearance—any one of these would have been sufficient to drown me in an ocean of despair. But I surprised myself with my own strength. Again, I thought this ability to withstand must be God's gift, a means to keep his human creation going through bad times. That, or maybe my strength came from my love for Jesse, which was a powerful engine indeed.

The morning was cool and foggy, yet I was sweating when we got close to home. Kitt sensed the nearness; her head went up and her step became less sloppy. I squeezed my eyes tight shut as we crested the hill that would at last afford us a glimpse of the farm. I clenched my jaw, steeling myself for the spectacle of a smoking ruin as monument to what was. But no! My heart rejoiced at the sight of our precious two-story frame house, gleaming white in the fog, splendid as any maharaja's palace!

"It's there, Pa!" I cried over my shoulder. "The Yanks did not burn us!"

They had visited us, though. The doors to the house and barn were wide open, and sweet Eugenie was nowhere in sight. Probably she inhabited some Yankee's stewpot.

I jumped to the ground and ran for the house; Jesse swung down from his horse and stopped me, holding me up off the ground as my legs pumped the air.

"Let me go!" I said, kicking. "Let me go, damn it! I need to see my house—I need to know what they did to us!"

"Wait, Hattie," Jesse said in a quiet voice, his mouth close to my ear. "Wait. We don't know it's safe, if they're gone. Let me go first, all right?"

What he said made sense, but I could not stop struggling. I was like out of my head, bucking and scratching like a catamount. Even though it was Jesse holding me, I felt I had to get free. Jess laughed a little and that made me all the wilder.

"I never believed what they say about red-heads 'till now! Stop it, Hattie! If the Yanks are still here they'll hear you."

I did like he said. I was played out, an empty vessel. When Jesse set me down, I flopped full length on the grass like a rag doll.

"Hellfire, let them shoot me," I said. "I don't care."

Jesse drew his revolver from his belt.

"Stay here," he said. "I'll let you know when it's safe to come on."

He walked through the fog toward the house, gun in hand, and disappeared through the front door. I stayed flat on my back staring at the morning sky. It would be the kind of day when the fog would burn off and leave in its place a beautiful Indian summer afternoon, warm and bright with sun. But would I enjoy this or any fine September day ever again? There I lay, awash in self-pity, when a familiar brown face appeared above me.

Earl Smith, stinking like a polecat and covered with stick burrs!

Filthy though he was, I was overcome at the sight of him. I hugged him to my chest and rolled with him in the dewy grass as he squirmed and licked my face with doggy joy.

"Earl," I said. "I thought you'd gone and got yourself killed like everybody else!"

He rewarded me with one of his most radiant smiles.

Jesse interrupted this happy reunion by stepping out onto the porch and waving the all-clear. Earl and I ran to the house, where Jesse received some Earl love almost equal to mine. The damage was bad but not ruinous. The windows were broken of course, our clothes and bedding stolen or shredded, the cellar robbed of all it contained but for one bag of cornmeal and a jar of mincemeat. What the Yankees didn't take was smashed on the floor. The devils even made off with every bit of Pa's plank fencing, leaving only the post holes. Still, we had the house and a roof for our heads. Also I found my inheritance earbobs and grandmother's lapis lazuli cameo. These thieves did not leave them out of compassion—like Pony, the harelip Jayhawker, so long ago—but because they overlooked the hidey hole where I stashed them.

First thing I did after checking the house and settling Pa was to cover Doak's grave with broken glass to discourage the flesh-eaters. After, Jess spoke a few words of comfort over Doak's earthly remains. He recited a Psalm as best he could from memory since the Rood family Bible was stolen by the Yankees, though what those devils wanted it for I could not imagine. Probably they'd use the pages to wipe their backsides.

Jesse apologized for the inadequacy of his recitation.

"Too bad Buck ain't here since he knows Scripture. Me, I never studied it, I didn't have the patience. But Frank, he'd sit and read for hours. The Bible and Shakespeare, too. Ma's awful proud of that."

We spent the day cleaning up and salvaging what we could. The day did not pan out like I expected; the fog lifted, but it stayed cool till dark and then it went flat-out cold. Although me and Jess covered the windows with newspaper and whatever else we could find, it was an ice house anyhow. We had no firewood, so Jesse busted up Doak's chiffonier and we burned that in the parlor heat stove. Dinner was coffee along with the last of our oatcakes and saltpork.

We ate on the floor by the stove. Our meal was right sorry, but the flames burning behind the isinglass panel on the stove door threw a nice orange light, making the parlor seem almost cozy.

"Hattie, I knew you had sand all along, but I know it double now, after these last few days," Jesse said. "I admire you for it."

"Well, thank you anyhow, but I guess I wish life required less sand from a girl. I fear my supply is near exhausted."

Here Jesse surprised me by leaning in and kissing me full on the mouth, even though it was full of oatcake.

"You'll make it," he said. "I know it. The Yanks have handed you a full ration of woe and suffering, but you don't let it finish you. You've got pluck, Hattie Rood, to a degree that is rare in a woman. The woman I marry will have such pluck."

Was there meaning in this remark? I thought so and decided therefore to be forthright.

"Jesse James, just how do you figure on making a living when this war ends?" It was a question that had been much on my mind. "How do you plan to support that plucky woman of yours? There won't be much demand for bushwhackers."

Jesse frowned and took a pull on his coffee.

"This war ain't going to end, not for me anyhow, not till the South wins. Way it looks, that may be some time."

"I think you're wrong," I said, surprising myself with my strength of feeling. "I think this war will be over in a year and the Yanks will win it. Everything we've fought for will be gone and Missouri won't never be the same. People like me and you, we'll need to find a new place in the world. I have an idea about that too."

I told him then about Montana Territory, of the riches there just for the taking. Thinking this would appeal to him, I told about how you got to the gold fields by following roads made by adventurers like John Bozeman and the mountain man Jim Bridger. I told him about the high snowy mountains and icy, trout-filled streams, about the Sioux and Cheyenne Indians—who could make it hot for white pilgrims —but how we would have the advantage because no place could be too hot for people like us from Missouri. He listened closely.

"So you've been thinking about this for some time, have you, Hattie?"

Yes, I had.

"And you think that's the answer for people like you and me?"

Yes, I did.

"What about the Yankees and what they did to your family? They killed your brothers, Hattie, both of 'em, and made your Pa simple." He looked to the far wall where Pa lay under blankets on a corn shuck mattress. "Don't any of that matter to you? Are you willing to just forget all that?"

Yes again. I wanted to forget it and in Montana I thought I might be able to.

"Well, that's where me and you are different. Me, I got to make them pay. Us Jameses worked hard to build ourselves up. We had a good farm, two hundred seventy-five acres, a family of nigras to help work it. Now Ma and them can't hardly get by!"

Jesse's blue eyes lit up like they did in moments of consuming passion.

"See, Hattie, I took an oath too, not like Frank's, but different. I swore my allegiance to Bill Anderson and the Brotherhood of Death. And like I said, I stand by my word."

I'd heard of Blue Lodges and the Sons of the South, but the Brotherhood of Death, now that was a new one.

"Is that so!" I said. "Do you boys have a secret sign or handshake? Maybe a password like all right on the hemp? Or sound on the goose?" These were the well-known "secret" phrases Blue Lodgers used to identify themselves.

But Jesse did not find this comical.

"I swore to avenge the death of any brother, no matter how he is killed, or when or where. We drew blood on it. So you see, I have lots of work to do."

Now I was serious too.

"Missouri's seen enough of that kind of work, Jesse James. The Good Lord put us here for something other than killing and stealing and burning. That is played out! I've had my fill of that kind of work and then some! Me, I'm going someplace different. I am going to Montana and if you had any sense you'd come with me!"

I embarrassed myself by crying. Jesse touched my face, pushing my hair back from my eyes.

"You're tired. Hattie. Let's not talk about this now. Go to sleep. Go on. I'll keep watch over you and your Pa."

I was tired, too tired to argue. I curled up on Ma's settee and Jesse put his coat over me for a blanket. Last thing I saw was his profile against the isinglass, cleaning his gun by its orange light.

Chapter Twenty-four

Although it was dangerous to remain at the house, there was no place for us to go. Pa was getting weaker and so thin it hurt to look at him. Me and Jess were skinny too. Jesse's Indian cheekbones looked sharp enough to cut through the flesh.

Hoe cakes and mincemeat held us for a day, but we needed fresh meat. Early the second morning Jess shouldered Pa's shotgun to hunt us some. In his belt he wore two revolvers.

"Come with me, why don't you?" he said. "You shouldn't be here alone."

I wanted to, but I couldn't.

"I won't be alone," I said. "I've got Pa and Earl for company."

He smiled halfway.

"That's so. Anyhow, I left a pistol in the parlor under the settee. It's loaded, just in case. I won't be gone long."

After he left, the quiet got so loud I couldn't hardly think. Anytime I did hear something, any little sound, I jumped clean out of my skin. To calm myself I decided to take a bath. God knew I needed one.

I dragged the tub from the pantry into the kitchen, found some verbena-scented bath powders tucked away in a corner and filled the tub with water heated on the stove till it was hot as I could take it. When I climbed in, my skin went all to gooseflesh and my muscles started melting like they were made of candle wax. I settled slowly in the water, savoring each inch of depth, letting the healing heat loosen my shoulders, my spine, my aching neck. Finally I immersed myself entire, head, hair, and scalp, then lathered my hair and body with sweet lemon soap. When I stepped from the water the suds left floating on the surface were brown in color, liked I'd just bathed a dog or a pony. After, I dressed in my faded but clean red calico. I felt like a new girl, pretty even.

Jess still wasn't back, so I heated more water and washed what few clothes we had. Pa could not help soiling himself, but even with all his things my laundering did not take long. Though overcast, the day was dry and warm and the laundry would dry quick. I might have clean clothes for Jesse when he got home. Maybe he'd like a bath too.

As I hung the wash on the line, I entertained myself with impure thoughts about me and Jesse and what I wanted to happen between us. I was thinking we were past the stage where I had to withhold myself from him to convince him I wasn't like the other women he might have known. I was thinking my womanly charms and our holy love for each other might be enough to entice him to a new life in Montana. I was thus engaged when two horsemen appeared on the river pike. Earl bristled, but I commanded him to stay. Our visitors wore blue, but they weren't Yankees. I could tell that right off.

They turned off the turnpike and started down the road to our house. They kept on coming instead of stopping at a distance and helloing the house as was custom. I recognized the smaller of the two as Archie, the Indian torturer from the bushwhacker camp. The other was a handsome fellow, wiry as whip leather, wearing the gold-braided coat and hat of a Federal officer. He rode a splendid black horse, tall as a Percheron, with silky tassels swinging from its bridle.

I dropped the camisole I was pinning back into the basket. A fist of fear tightened in my belly as the two urged their horses forward. As they drew near, I realized the dark rider was familiar too; he was on the Richmond road the day Cy was killed. He was the one Archie addressed as captain, the one who ordered the execution of the Yankee officer. I told myself to calm down, trying to master my pounding heart. These fellows were Jesse's friends. There was no cause to worry.

Archie stopped his horse as his companion dismounted. He handed Archie the reins and started toward me with a friendly smile. His eyes were pale gray, his beard neatly trimmed, and his dark, curling hair fell to his shoulders. When he got close, he doffed his plumed hat with a flourish and bent at the waist, like an actor on a stage. His small feet were encased in black boots of polished kid.

"You must be pretty red-haired Hattie," he said in a honey voice. "I've heard a good deal about you and only good things." His smile made me think of butter sliding off a biscuit.

"I am Hattie Rood," I said.

His eyes slipped from me to the house, the barn, the privy. Leaves skittered across the brown grass. Our place presented a desolate scene, even to my loving eyes.

"It appears you've had some trouble here, Hattie."

"That don't make us special in this neighborhood," I said.

He nodded sadly.

"True enough, though still I am sorry for your inconvenience. These are hard times we're living in. Very hard times."

He paused like he expected me to acknowledge this jewel of wisdom, but I didn't. When a thing is plain it don't require saying.

"Anyhow," he said, "I came by to speak to your father. Where is Captain Rood, Hattie?"

His eyes went sly as a wolf's.

My fear was growing stronger by the second, but I knew it would be a bad mistake to show fear to this man in the same way you don't show it to a horse or a mean dog. It was a struggle, though. My heart was thumping so loud and hard I felt sure he could hear it.

"Pa's out in the field," I said. "Hoping the Yanks left us

some to get by on. I'll tell him you came by, Mister..."

"Oh?" He raised his eyebrows. "Your Pa's in the field?" His smile deepened and he gestured over his shoulder at Archie. "I'm surprised to hear it. My associate, Mr. Clement, says the old man is poorly. Unable to walk even."

Despite my heart, my voice was calm when I answered.

"Well, if you knew that why'd you ask me?"

He lost his buttery smile.

"You are very insolent, Miss Rood. A Southern girl should show respect to a cavalier fighting on her behalf."

You bushwhackers are fighting on your own hook and for yourselves only. I thought this, but I did not say it. This man was so very dangerous.

His eyes ran the length of my body, making my skin crawl. His gaze was the caress of a grave-cold hand. Then he stepped forward and took me by the arm. Bending in close, he buried his face in my hair and inhaled deeply.

"You smell of lemons, Hattie," he said. "You smell like the sweet lemon cakes my mother made for us when we were children. Oh, those were happy days, so different from what we have now."

He stood back but did not release my arm.

"You know," he said, "suddenly I am hungry. *You*, pretty Hattie, you make me hungry. Let's go inside, shall we? Perhaps we'll find something there inside the house that might satisfy me. Do you think so, Hattie?"

Little Archie giggled as he urged the horses forward.

"He's hungry, Hattie," Archie said. "Very hungry."

Alarm bells rang in my head as I let the tall stranger lead me to the house.

I fought the impulse to run, knowing there was no running from these two. My only hope was to get Jesse's revolver from under the settee. Somehow I had to get to it before they did.

"You stay out here, Arch," the dark man said to the pygmy when we reached the porch. "Tie up the horses and keep an eye on the road. Don't interrupt us unless it's important. Miss Rood and I wish to be alone."

Archie giggled again as my captor held the door for me to enter. When I hesitated, he pushed me roughly into the parlor. I broke free and faced him, shaking uncontrollably with fear and fury. Suddenly I knew who he was. Why hadn't I known him before?

"You are Bill Anderson!"

"At your service."

He inclined his head in a formal fashion, like he was asking for the next dance at a cotillion.

"This is a sorry way to repay Pa's kindness," I said.

Anderson glanced dismissively at poor Pa, curled up on a straw tick on the floor. He shrugged his shoulders.

"It's your own fault, my dear." He dropped his hat and began to unbutton his blue jacket. "I came here with the best intentions, but you riled me with your insolence."

Panicked, I dove for the floor and lunged for Jesse's revolver, but Anderson was on me in an instant, gripping me in arms that were strong as iron. The more I fought, the tighter his grasp. Finally I stopped, knowing struggle was futile. He lay on top of me, his face inches from mine, his long black hair brushing my face. Despite his fine appearance his breath was rotten, like meat left in the sun, and his gray eyes were cold and inhuman. Nothing I could do or say would touch this man, I saw that clear enough, so I closed my eyes and braced for the horror to come.

"Leave her be, Bill."

It was Jesse's voice. He had entered the house from the kitchen, avoiding Archie on the porch, and stood in the hallway with a pistol in his hand. Anderson froze, then released me and got slowly to his feet. In an instant I was up off the floor and at Jesse's side.

Anderson was unruffled. He smiled, cool as ever you please.

"Why, Dingus," he said. "Look at you. You're recovered

—more than I was led to believe."

"I don't want to shoot you, Bill," Jesse said. "You know it. But I can't let you hurt her."

Anderson raised his eyebrows.

"I expected different from you, laddie my lad. Why, just yesterday I was bragging on you to the boys. The 'keenest and cleanest fighter in the command' I said of you, and now this..."

He shook his curly head in an exaggerated show of disappointment. Then his wolf eyes narrowed and gestured toward the porch.

"You know what Archie will do to you if you shoot me? What he'll do to pretty Hattie here?"

Jess nodded.

"I know it. But it don't change nothing. I won't let you hurt her."

Anderson reflected a moment, his head cocked to the side. Then he picked up his hat, slapped it against his leg, and put it on at a rakish angle.

"I'll say this for you, Dingus. You've got sand and there's nothing I admire more in a man. This act of defiance could have cost you your life. I suppose the girl means something to you."

With this, the beast who just moments before threatened me with grievous harm actually winked at me, playful as a pup!

"So," Anderson continued, "for that, and as a favor to your brother, I am inclined to let this incident pass. In fact, today is a special day, a day for celebration. That indeed is the reason I'm here. The liberation of Missouri has begun! Sterling Price is on the move with three divisions under Fagan, Marmaduke and Shelby. Frank wanted to come with me today to tell you the news, but I made him stay back to ready the boys. I shall take my men east to occupy the Federals north of the Missouri and oh!" He pumped his fist in the air. "We will give them hell! I want you with me, Jesse. I meant it when I said you are the keenest fighter in my command. Hurry on if you aim to share the glory!"

He spun on his heel and quit the room, letting the door slam behind him. Only then did I succumb to my terror. My knees buckled and I sank to the floor. Jesse knelt beside me.

"Are you all right?" he asked.

I nodded. "Thank God you came when you did. Otherwise..." A shudder, more like a convulsion, ran through me.

"It wasn't God that saved you," he said. "It was that dog of yours came for me. Earl. He found me, let me know I was supposed to follow him."

I nodded. Nothing surprised me anymore.

"I've got to go with him, Hattie," Jesse said. For a moment I was confused, thinking he meant Earl.

"It pains me to leave you in this hole, but I've got to join Bill and the boys. I've got to."

I guess life did hold a few more surprises for me, for this rocked me to my core.

"Join him? You can't mean it! You can't mean to ride with that devil after what just happened! Now you know the kind of man he is! You're not like that, Jesse, you know you aren't! Me and you, I thought we were going to Montana."

Jesse shook his head.

"Hattie, I never said that. That was all your idea. Much as I care for you, I have allegiance to the cause and my family. Frank is with Bill and we stick together. That's how it is."

Unbelieving, I followed him up to the loft where he began packing his things. It seemed so long ago that I tended him in this hot box, when his hold on life was so fragile. Now that he was strong he was leaving me! How cruel! What a heartless way to reward my devotion!

"Don't go, Jess," I said miserably. My pride deserted me, or maybe it was the other way around. Whichever, me and it parted company. "Please don't go."

He didn't say anything but pulled a photograph out of his saddle bag and put it in my hands. It was a likeness of him, unsmiling and wearing a cavalier's hat pinned up on the side. He held a Colt Patterson in his right hand and two other pistols were tucked in his belt. On it he had inscribed in pencil the words: "To Hattie, who saved me. Jesse."

"That picture was made in Platte City this summer," he said. "Keep it to remember me by. I'll be back when all this is over. I promise."

Then he bent down. A feeling rose up in me, a wildness akin to desperation. He kissed me. It was not how I had imagined my first experience, it was not a spring evening, there were no candles or gauzy gowns or fresh white sheets, there was no bed. But Jesse was sweet and attentive. In my heart, I became Jesse's wife that day: Thursday, September 22, 1864.

I never saw him again.

Epilogue

You may be surprised to learn that I will end my days in New York City in a fine Park Avenue apartment. No one is more surprised by the way things turned out than me. I am not unhappy, far from it, though the particulars of this final chapter are not exactly as I would have them, were it up to me. But my son decides things for me nowadays and I mostly go along. Few things peeve me, now I am old.

I do have one persistent vexation, however, and that is the Widow Custer, who resides in my building on the floor below. That woman is a bee in my bonnet. She galls me no end. The doorman makes a great to-do over her and people frequently ask for her autograph. Despite her advanced age— and she is even older than I am!—she is vain as can be and queens around like she is still the belle of the regiment. She is sad and ridiculous, yet I recognize we have something in common, me and the Widow Custer: we were once loved by remarkable men, men who made history. Never will I use the word *great* to describe the Yankee George Custer, a vainglorious rooster if ever there was one, and I know many folks will never use that word together with the name of Jesse James. But no one can deny those two were big men, bigger than most.

Despite his promise, Jesse did not come back for me. Why, I will never know for sure, though I have ideas. So much happened in the fall of 1864 to forever change the course of our lives. Just days after Jesse left, Bill Anderson led his men on a bloody massacre in Centralia that resulted in the murder of twenty-five unarmed Union soldiers. The newspapers said Bloody Bill and his boys gunned those fellows down as they stood in a pitiful line, naked, begging for their lives. It was a shameful and cowardly act, one that sickened all Missourians and helped turn the tide of public sentiment against the bushwhackers for the remainder of the war. Anderson was killed in Ray County on October 27th by Missouri State Militia under Lieutenant Colonel Samuel P. Cox, who will forever be a hero to a good many Show-me Staters, Northern and Southern alike. They took Bloody Bill's body into Richmond, photographed it, and displayed it in the courthouse, where hundreds of people filed by to see it, though I was not among them. After, his defiled remains were buried in the cemetery outside of town and for years to come men made a pilgrimage to the grave for the satisfaction of urinating on it. I bet they still do.

Only when reading of Anderson's death did I learn the silky tassels I saw hanging from his horse's bridle that terrible day were human scalps.

Some say Jesse took part in the Centralia business and the battle that followed. John Newman Edwards, a notorious drunkard and prevaricator, wrote it was Jesse himself who shot Union Major Ave Johnston pointblank on the battlefield, and Frank James backed Edwards in that claim. Me, I refuse to believe Jesse would abide the murder of unarmed men. If Jesse was in Centralia that day, and I say if, I know in my heart he had nothing to do with that dreadful business. And if he shot Johnston, it would have been in self-defense.

As for all the tales of banditry that followed, the robbing of banks and trains and so forth, I suppose Jesse may have done some of these things—certainly not all laid at his feet— but not for money or material gain. If Jesse stole, if he killed, he did so through allegiance to the Brotherhood of Death, like he told me about that afternoon in the parlor. That's how I see it.

My personal story was less eventful. Joe Craighead and I married on Christmas Eve, 1864. Ours was a small ceremony, attended only by members of Joe's family and Fritz Heizinger, the German neighbor who brought Jesse into my life by wounding him that August afternoon. After the war, me and Joe settled in St. Louis, finding a place for Pa in Soldiers' Home, where he spent hours rocking on the porch. He seemed content enough, though he never recovered from the brain seizure or whatever it was that afflicted him the night of Doak's death. He was well cared for there, even though he lived for only two years after my marriage.

Earl Smith astonished us all by holding on another ten. He must have been only a pup that day me and Doak found him by the river, blindfolded and mostly dead. He was ever the sweetest and most amiable of companions. I've had many dogs in my life but never one to match him. How could I? He was with me during my most desperate hours.

Joe had a good head for business, and his mercantile prospered after the war. We left the Richmond store for the one-legged clerk, Harley Thomas, to manage, and opened a new one in St. Louis which succeeded beyond even Joe's expectations. We bought a fine brick home on Gratiot Street just a stone's throw from the spot where the dreaded women's prison once stood. Earl never did get used to the big house and passed most of his days sitting by the tall windows in the front room, looking out on the busy street. Often I wondered if he wasn't searching for old Kitt or Eugenie, or waiting for Pa and the boys to come in from the fields.

I never saw Montana. My son would take me if I asked him, but it might not live up to my dream and that would take something precious from me, so I won't.

Joe and I had a good marriage and a long one. We did not discuss the old days. If he had questions, he did not ask and I did not offer. We had an unspoken agreement, I guess you could say, and it worked out all right for us. Together we raised five children, four daughters, all red-heads, and one boy we named John, after Pa. I was a loving mother but not a patient one, for I could not abide a whiner. My youngsters, the girls especially, learned to appeal to their father when they had a complaint because he was the softer of the two of us, especially where the girls were concerned.

Me, I was partial to my boy. For some reason I never warmed to his wife, my daughter-in-law, though I reckon she was all right. People say she favors me as a young woman, and maybe she does, but my daughter-in-law does not know the treasure she has in my son. She does not know and I cannot tell her.

Although grateful to Joe and my circumstances, I confess I kept looking for Jesse longer than I should have. Even after the Judas Bob Ford shot him from behind in 1882, part of me kept looking, for a time anyhow. It didn't make sense, but I simply could not believe one of those trashy Fords, a family of Ray County polecats, could finish Jesse James. I know many other people shared my opinion. I guess he did it, though.

I myself felt speared through the heart when I learned Jesse had married his cousin, Zee, a plain woman who nursed him back to health after he was shot through the chest (again!) in 1865. Oh, the roiling mix of emotion this knowledge stirred up in me! Did she nurse him in a loft? Did she hold his head as he drank, and did he thank her for her ministrations saying, "You have a gentle touch, Miss Zee?" Most of all I wonder did he see my face when he looked at her? I was much prettier, not a boast but true! I saw photographs of her in the newspapers at the time of Jesse's death. Why did he marry her? Was it because he heard I was with Joe? Of all the torments I have known, this notion of what might have been cuts the deepest.

Some others from those times I kept track of: giggling Archie Clement was gunned down on the streets of Lexington in December 1866; Ol Shepherd was killed by vigilantes at his father's house in 1868. Whatever became of Nat Tigue I can't tell you, although I am certain it wasn't good. Frank James and Cole Younger, both old men, went into the Wild West Show business after Cole got out of that Minnesota jail. The week the show came to St. Louis, the little boys ran up and down our street shooting off make-believe pistols and chanting:

> *Jesse's up from thunder,*
> *Which is near to County Clay—*
> *Jesse and the Younger boys*
> *Are galloping this way.*

I did not attend the show. I wasn't even tempted.

Jesse's photograph I kept tucked away in my underthings drawer where it was my secret treasure. The photo accompanied me on all my moves, including this final one to New York, where my boy, John, has a fine department store. New York is a splendid city, but it will never be home. I miss Missouri so, especially in the fall when I walk in Central Park searching the trees in vain for the bittersweet vines with their bright orange pods; nighttimes I long for the soothing buzz of cicada and the deep-throated croak of the river bullfrogs. In New York, the autumn air does not smell of apples or freshly mowed hay.

On those days I return to my apartment and take the picture from its place of hiding, which is now the roll top desk, the same one old man Craighead kept in the back room of his Richmond store. I hold it in my hands like a miser with his gold. Those are exquisite moments of pleasure and pain; their intensity has never diminished throughout the years. Even now, with my red hair gone coarse and gray and Jesse cold in his grave, I feel it still.

The day came when my son found the photograph. It was after Joe died and John came to St. Louis to move me to New York, closer to him and his family. He discovered it in a box I had marked Private Papers.

"Mother!" He called up the stairs to me in my bedroom where I was packing my clothes. "Mother, what is this?"

I knew immediately what he had found. I knew it from the sound of his voice. I walked down the stairs to the study, where he held the yellowing picture aloft. My heart throbbed like it did in the old days. Other than mine, his were the first eyes to behold it since the autumn day Jesse gave it to me half a century before.

He read aloud the inscription. "To Hattie, who saved me. Jesse."

I held onto the back of a chair to keep my knees from buckling.

"Mother, do you know who this is?"

I nodded.

"He was a friend from long ago." I was relieved that I could still master my voice when I had to. "From the Missouri days."

John looked at me in disbelief.

"A friend? Mother, this is Jesse James," he said.

"I know it."

He gave a short laugh and shook his head.

"Jesse James was your friend? My God, the man was a thief—an outlaw! What kind of company did you keep back then? What else haven't you told me?"

I smiled then, despite myself. My poor boy; he knew only the half of it. John never knew that every time I looked at him I saw his father, not the good man who raised him but his father, and he never would.

Gazing into my son's astonished blue eyes, eyes blue as cornflowers, I offered the only explanation I had.

"Those were fevered times," I said. "They made outlaws of us all."

He did not question me further, knowing I had nothing else to say. I am an honest woman but there is one secret, one lie, I will take with me to my grave.

Now my days are short and I await the end without fear—well, not much. In truth, the emotion I feel most of all is excitement. Will I see him again at last? Will he remember?